STRETCHED LOVE

Gordon Blitz

STRETCHED LOVE
by Gordon Blitz

ISBN: 978-1-958661-07-9

Tofu Ink Arts Press, a celebratory venture, aims at publishing poems
and other arts of un humdrum'd inclusive rhizomatic errant possibilities.
We support polished work of established & emerging poets and artists
that are absorbed in possibilities. We are committed to amplifying voices
of the under-represented and marginalized.
Art makes you think about thinking…
ABSORB POSSIBILITIES!

www.TOFUINK.com
A member of CLMP

For my friend Paul Furman

Acknowledgements

Luba for her proofing, my husband, Neal Wiener, for putting up with my writing obsession and Michael Main who patiently edited each word, helped me mold and shape the novel and made me laugh from his comments when I went into my full-diva mode.

This is a work of fiction. Unless otherwise indicated, all the names, characters, businesses, places, events and incidents in this book are either the product of the author's imagination or used in a fictitious manner. Any resemblance to actual persons, living or dead, or actual events is purely coincidental.

CONTENTS

Prologue

At first, Warren thought the energy force and faint odor had aroused him until he realized it was the smell of coffee. He thought, *thank you my love for remembering to set the Keurig so we'd have fresh caffeine in the morning.* Rebecca looked consumed with finishing eight hours of sleep. The Land End's Supima sheets wrapped around her frame, a blonde beauty queen resting. Last night's lovemaking had guaranteed an unencumbered sleep for both of them. After Warren edged out from Rebecca's spooning embrace, Rebecca curled into the fetal position. Warren's scratchy eyes searched for the bathroom to relieve himself. The itch on his shaft was disconcerting. The bathroom's marble tile cooled his feet and stretching his biceps energized Warren. He used his favorite oatmeal-colored washcloth to give himself a whore's bath, a quick sponge bath by hand. His stumpy fingertips needed rebandaging. He'd given up trying to break that habit of nail biting. He grabbed his cargo shorts and walked down the staircase to the main floor that housed the living and dining rooms along with the kitchen. He passed the rarely used front entrance at the end of the stairs because the kitchen had a door to the two-car garage in the back of the townhouse.

Since Rebecca had announced they were going to be parents last week, they'd been feasting on the thrill of having a child. Their shared DNA would create a testament to their values and love. With Rebecca's speech therapist position blocks away and Warren's office within five miles, their Ocean Garden townhouse was a jackpot winner of places to live. The cliché *it takes a village* took on a luscious meaning for them.

Sunday morning was Warren's favorite day. He would make gluten-free waffles smothered with Costco real maple syrup and blueberries. There was freshly ground Peet's coffee and pulpy Valencia orange juice. In the background, KUSC played the Mostly Mozart Program while they would read the Los Angeles Times.

Warren walked back to the second floor to awaken his wife, but she wasn't in bed. Warren listened for the shower in the second bedroom but it was silent. Outside the bathroom, he saw the remains of a pouch sitting open on the bathroom counter. An oddity since she was so careful to keep it germ-free.

"Rebecca, where are you?" He checked the walk-in closet hoping she was deciding what sumptuous outfit she would be wearing, but it was empty. Rebecca may have been surveying the grounds looking for ripening lemons, figs, oranges, limes or flowers. The birds of paradise were in abundance and would make a lovely centerpiece for the round teak dining room table.

Warren began checking out the sports section in the paper until Rebecca returned. Underneath the newspaper, Warren found a letter. The official-looking court return address intrigued Warren to read further. Ah yes, it was about a partnership Rebecca had invested in with her brother. The letter looked ominous. This was ancient history. He wondered if the letter upset Rebecca. He continued reading that there was going to be a distribution of the funds. Warren hadn't remembered how much money was tied up in the company, Realtor Plus. He was relieved that most of the inheritance from Rebecca's mom had supplied them with a healthy deposit on their townhouse.

After half an hour Warren decided to scan the complex for Rebecca's location. The seventy-five townhouses imitated Palm Springs because the semi-private road circling the perimeter of the community ensured no street noises. The road was used for guest parking while the common areas were within the circle. Ocean Garden was blessed by not being a gated community which pleased Rebecca and Warren's sensibilities. A gated community would have given them a false sense of security and jailed isolation.

The eerie quiet for a Sunday morning disturbed Warren. Even the pool was empty. Normally, Alexandra and Garth would perch themselves on the pool lounges and be engulfed in the New York Times by now. The tennis court was vacant.

Rebecca's disappearance was out of character. Warren grabbed his I-phone and tried calling her number. After eight rings it went to voicemail. Odd. Rebecca was always good about answering and leaving the ringer on. Jaunting back to the townhouse and hoping Rebecca had returned lightened Warren's mood. The radio was off and there was a man sitting at the dining room table.

"Oh, hi, Warren. I wondered what happened to you. I'm starving. Becky finally slept through the night. Thank goodness, her teething has stopped. I was hoping we could make love this morning."

"Who are you? Get out of here or I'm calling the police."

"What? It's Paul. Stop fooling around. You're getting me scared."

Warren imagined this was a hallucination. Not only was Rebecca missing but a strange man who pretended to be his lover was in the dining room who knew Warren's name. And how could there be a baby upstairs sleeping?

Warren said, "Where's Rebecca?"

Chapter 1
Rebecca and Warren

Rebecca loved living with her brother Paul in their Silverlake apartment while they both were attending Cal State Northridge. The bohemian neighborhood contrasted with their previous neurotic West Hollywood home base with their mom. The harmonious mixture of Gay, Latino, Asian, Black and White gave diversity an A-plus. Serious gentrification hadn't raised its ugly head yet. Paul was a sublime roommate. A stereotypical gay male who was sweetly sex obsessed, a gourmet top chef, a connoisseur of Marc Jacobs' fashion and Martha Stewart organization skills. Paul's only flaw was his hypocritical daily quest of wanting her to seriously date while he continued to be a serial sex maniac.

He pleaded with her, "I want you to meet this man. He's got these melting hazel eyes, velvety skin when he shaves, and he's muscle-bound."

"Sounds like your type, Paul."

"You know I don't have a type. He's very straight and going to be a lawyer."

"I hate lawyers. Why would I want to go out with a lawyer?"

"Because he'll make you laugh. He's the happiest person I know. I'm tired of you moping around. When was the last time you even went out on a date?"

Rebecca despised dating. She was still smarting from the collapse of her first love from Fairfax High School. Warren had been swooning over her since tenth grade. He had that *"I know I'm good-looking"* attitude that plugged up her attraction. But in eleventh grade, he stole Rebecca's confused breath when she saw him running track, naked from the waist up. His sculptured chest rippled during the mile race. Each muscular definition waved at Rebecca. The curly hair that topped his head begged to be petted. Warren's face exploded with masculine bravura defined by deep set eyes coupled with edible lips. He had ignored her until she watched Warren perform on the debate team. His bass voice captivated her attention. In 1999 his team was passionately supporting George Bush.

"Big government is a recipe for disaster. Private industry does a much better job of running things. I don't want Government controlling my life. Our founding fathers believed in freedom from tyranny. If you vote for Al Gore it will be more in the same direction as the Clinton mess. Clinton was a disgrace. Impeached for lying to Congress. We need a change from the liberal policies that are ruining this country."

Rebecca was repulsed by his conservative views until he later told her, "I was assigned to represent Republican views. I don't believe any of that crap." Rebecca and Warren opened the floodgates of emotions. They clung to each other during Warren's senior year. Rebecca finished his sentences informing him that they had been lovers in a previous life. Her probing cat-eyes and the fetching way she flipped hair off her forehead turned Warren into a Rebecca addict. His failure to find an imperfection left him a helpless lover under her spell. Yet a surprise element pushed him over the top.

She had just turned seventeen when she told eighteen-year-old Warren, "I want you to make love to me." Warren's virginity held in a gasp when he heard her words and quietly responded, "I would be honored for you to be the first woman I make love to." This last grasp before Warren left for San Diego State had created closure for their geographical separation. Rebecca's open-minded parents allowed her to take The Pill, and as an extra precaution, Warren would use a Trojan condom. Warren sprung for a room at Shutters in Santa Monica. He wanted the night of a thousand stars to be a triumph and to awaken to a killer view of the Pacific Ocean. The planets aligned themselves so orgasms were attained within minutes of each other, after languorous foreplay that began with the licking of each other's toes and fingers, clearing the way for a massage, before a stitch of clothing was removed. Simultaneous carnal knowledge. After their first tryst, Rebecca explained to Warren about having simultaneous orgasms and what that would entail. The patient teacher and eager student accomplished that feat a month after their marriage. Rebecca and Warren liked to think that they were the only couple in the world that celebrated that achievement!

They burned through the summer of 1999 before their first separation arrived at the tail end of August. Warren kept reiterating, "It's only a year. When you graduate, we can live together. San Diego is only a two-hour drive. We'll still get to see each other on the weekend." Her heart was knifed on the fatal day he drove away.

John Irving's *The World According to Garp* saved Rebecca while she languished in her mom's West Hollywood Formosa Street apartment. Her escape into John Irving's environment distracted her from Warren's departure.

The daily phone chatting softened the anguish of the first Monday through Friday detachment. At the end of the first week after Warren's departure, Rebecca woke to wet bed sheets. She screamed looking at blisters covering every inch of her mouth in the bathroom mirror. A crushing exhaustion of aches was circumventing her body. Panicking after reaching a temperature of 102, she immediately sought medical advice. The urgent plea enabled her primary care physician, Dr. Resnick, to squeeze Rebecca into her tight schedule. After examining her corrupted mouth, she said, "Have you had oral sex recently? These things usually happen seven days after contact. It appears that you've contracted herpes. It's not deadly. Just a nuisance and you will be very contagious right before an outbreak. I'll send a prescription to your pharmacy."

Rebecca enveloped herself into a horror mode. She had spent the night with Warren a week ago as a departing gift to each other. Rebecca couldn't believe that Warren had infected her. He said he was a virgin. Was he lying? She dialed his number and got voicemail, "Please call me back. I need to talk to you." Her voice fumed as she left the message.

Rebecca's mouth was on fire. Eruptions were making eating become a foul exercise. The doctor had warned her that the first outbreak was excruciating. She was embarrassed to reveal this diagnosis to friends and she didn't want to frighten her frail widowed mother. Rebecca had been a change-of-life baby and her mom was a newly minted early senior citizen. The twenty-year difference between Mom and her father Michael created a lopsided relationship with Rebecca. Mom flipped between wife and caregiver. Her father attained a puzzling grandfather status. When she talked about Mariah Carey, Meatloaf, women's rights, Starbucks, and AIDS he looked at her like an out-of-space visitor. With his heart angina, Rebecca feared detonating him with thoughts about boys or cultural references foreign to him. His right-wing politics threw most subjects off the Formica table. Dad died soon after Rebecca turned anything but sweet sixteen.

Rebecca never saw her mom cry after Dad died. They had been married for forty years. She never saw them argue and assumed they had a good marriage despite the generation gap. The lack of weeping confounded Rebecca. When Rebecca howled before her father's funeral, Edna pulled her aside and told her, "I know you are in pain. You've lost your father. I've lost my husband. But crying isn't going to help you. Your father would want you to be strong. He wouldn't want you to fall apart. It's just the three of us now. So, promise me, no more crying." The seeds of isolation were in play. She only allowed her tears to be unleashed with her brother. Rebecca and Paul knotted together with a daily ritual of "I love you." They continued the custom for the rest of their lives.

Recently Edna was no longer the rock of Gibraltar. So, Rebecca tiptoed around any alarms that would trigger Mom's concern. Her plan had been to share an apartment with her younger brother Paul in a year. He was skipping a semester to graduate early from Hollywood High so that Edna could scale down her lifestyle and move to a senior independent living situation in Beach Woods. Rebecca didn't want to add any drama to Edna's plans. Paul's intention to attend Cal State Northridge would enable sister and brother to not only be roommates but also carpool.

Warren needed to respond quickly to quiet Rebecca's angry voicemail. They had never fought and this confrontation frightened her love for Warren. Her cell phone mustered seven rings before she accepted the call.

"Hi, Rebecca. You sounded so distraught on your message. Are you okay?"

"Oh, God, Warren. I have herpes all over my mouth. I'm in agony and the doctor thinks I picked it up from you. Tell me that isn't true."

Warren's pause was a ticking explosion in Rebecca's head.

"I don't have herpes. I may have gotten a cold sore when I was a kid but nothing like what you're talking about. What else did the doctor say?"

"That it takes seven days after you've been with a contagious partner. We had sex a week before this outbreak."

The longer pause jumpstarted Rebecca's heart.

Warren quietly said, "I'm sorry but it didn't come from me. Tell me what to do to help you."

"Are you saying I picked this up from someone else?"

"I don't have herpes."

Rebecca didn't believe him and replied, "I don't know what to do. I can't talk. I'm in too much pain."

She dropped the call, ignoring his, "I love you."

Rebecca called Dr. Resnick to relieve her gnawing anxiety.

"I asked my boyfriend if he infected me, and he said he's never had herpes. He did say he had cold sores as a child but had outgrown them. How did this happen to me?"

She gently responded, "He may be asymptomatic. The virus never leaves your system. It can lay dormant for years. So, he still could have infected you. If you like he should go to his physician and get tested. I hope your pain is better and the medication should relieve the oozing."

Rebecca redialed Warren and asked him to get tested. He agreed and repeated, "I love you." Rebecca was unable to respond. She was convinced Warren had damaged her.

When her mom insisted on serving her spaghetti and meatballs, she was unable to go beyond two bites. Edna ignored Rebecca's squished face and nausea and blankly stared at the yellowed linoleum floor. Her gingerly shuffling as she left the kitchen worried Rebecca. She'd been reading about early signs of dementia and that type of walking might be a precursor. The second floor without an elevator building wouldn't allow Rebecca any tranquility until Edna moved to the one-floor apartments in Beach Woods.

"Mom, I just don't have an appetite. Just wrap it up. I'll eat it for lunch tomorrow."

Two days passed before Warren called, "Sorry, Rebecca, I've been so busy getting acclimated to my dorm mates. I've never shared a room with anyone before and this guy's a major slob. I was so worried that I had the virus and infected you, but I did take the test and it was negative. I feel so horrible."

"I don't believe you. My doctor said you could be asymptomatic and still infect me."

"But Rebecca I don't have herpes. You know I would never do anything to hurt you. I was fine. I mean I am fine. I know I said I would come back this weekend but there is too much going on here. This first week was a killer. I promise we'll get together the following week."

Rebecca's body had been contaminated. Warren's excuse felt disingenuous. Rebecca wanted him to come back to West Hollywood and cleanse her. Make her believe him. Where was the unvarnished love?

A polluted passivity came from her swollen mouth, "That's okay, Warren. I understand." Rebecca's misery continued with another health trauma. Her stomach rebelled with painful gas and repeated trips to the bathroom.

There was no reunion. Warren had excuses for not trekking back to Los Angeles. And he never asked Rebecca to visit him. He told her, "I only have a single bed. There would be no place for you to sleep. My roommate Elijah is always around and we would have no privacy. Plus, I'm working at Jamba Juice on the weekend."

"Why are you working? I thought your parents were paying your tuition."

"Money is really tight since both my parents are sick with cancer, and I don't want to be saddled with a student loan. Room and board are more expensive than we thought. Look, it will be Thanksgiving in no time. We can spend four glorious days together."

Before Rebecca hung up, she said, "Warren, I need to go. I've got another doctor's appointment."

Rebecca strangled all communication with Warren. She deleted emails and phone messages. Followed by ripping up letters from Warren. She instructed her mother, "I've broken up with Warren. I don't want to talk to him. No matter how much he begs, don't let him in the apartment." Mom had become complacent and didn't question her daughter's decision.

Her best friend from kindergarten, Jackie, kept asking Rebecca what was going on with Warren. Despite taking a blood pact at age ten, Rebecca feared revealing her herpes diagnosis. She lied to Jackie, "I found out he was seeing Susan Duke. That stuck-up bitch."

"Isn't she in college?"

"Yes, I can't believe Warren would go out with her. Such a cliché about guys being into older women. I hate him."

Rebecca compartmentalized her lies. The security blanket of honesty with Jackie had been broken because she wouldn't reveal the real reason for the busted relationship. This was the first secret that Rebecca buried. Rebecca had told Jackie the details of making love to Warren and even when and how she masturbated. She swore to herself, "This is the last time I'll ever keep anything from Jackie."

On Thanksgiving, the family rendezvoused at their gay Uncle Buddy's in Silverlake. His three-bedroom apartment overlooked the lake and each room had a personality. The art deco bedroom had wall-to-wall Man Ray photos and walnut veneer furniture. The second bedroom was stuck in the 1960s from the pink princess phone to framed posters of favorite films from that era; *Funny Girl, Bonnie and Clyde,* and *2001 A Space Odyssey.* The floor treatment of gold shag completed the room with a Shelly sofa. The authentic Victorian living and dining room felt like they were in Merry Olde England. During the Christmas celebratory dinner, they expected carolers to pop out from the walls while they ate roast beef and Yorkshire pudding.

Buddy was Rebecca and Paul's favorite relative and being an out gay man was a perfect role model for Paul. Edna's gut told her that Paul might be gay after they saw the film *Victor Victoria* on television in 1995. The story of a poverty-stricken singer played by Julie Andrews who pretends to be a man performing as a female was a fairy tale musical.

He told his mom, "I loved the Robert Preston character. He's just like Uncle Buddy. I want to be just like him. He gets to dress up like a girl and sing. And I love Julie Andrews."

When her older brother Buddy came out to her in 1988 it was a non-event. Edna's career as a hospice nurse made her tolerant on the road to unconditional acceptance. Years of witnessing the love between same-sex couples during end-of-life care made her realize love had no boundaries. She had listened to endless stories of the shame her gay patients felt. The common disowning by their parents riddled her with anger. Edna's listening skills were mythic. Edna embraced her role of escorting men as they transitioned, never fearing infection while she held their emaciated flesh.

Edna's fear about Buddy catching the virus was suppressed when he told her, "I'm practically a monk and when I do have sex it's very vanilla."

Edna responded, "I don't think I want to know what that means, but as long as you are safe, I'm happy."

Edna called Buddy after the *Victor Victoria* episode, "Buddy, I just had the most interesting conversation with Paul. I know he's only thirteen but I think it's time for the talk. Look, he's always hanging around with his boyfriends. So many sleepovers either here or at their house."

'Edna, don't you think it's too soon? You don't really know."

"I know, Buddy. A mother has an ingrained sense. I've seen him trying on my makeup."

"If that's what you want. I know you are worried about AIDS. At least he's good at sports. Something I never tackled and was bullied constantly because of it."

Buddy started mentoring Paul and it gave Edna a sense of relief. Buddy needed a vacation from the barrage of AIDS memorial services he had attended in the last ten years. Thank God the virus had dissipated in 1996 and cocktails to prevent further ravages of the AIDS virus were the rage.

After Thanksgiving stomach-stuffing and Edna napping in Buddy's study, Rebecca told her brother and Buddy the details about the breakup with Warren. Herpes and his chicken shit response. Both agreed with her decision to disable Warren from contacting her. She focused on graduating and her college track of being a Speech Language Pathologist (SLP). The news that her friend, Jackie, got swept along with her decision and planned to attend Cal State Northridge with a speech major, provided solace to Rebecca.

Rebecca didn't choose speech therapy as her major; speech therapy picked *her*. In second grade, vocal communication came to a halt. Mom tried tricking her to speak by incessantly asking her questions that begged for answers, "Rebecca, what kind of ice cream do you want? What television show should we watch, Sesame Street or Mr. Rogers? Which dress do you want to wear?" Rebecca shook her head or ignored her mom. She shut down, petrified of using her voice. Rebecca's second-grade teacher, Mrs. Gerrick, called, "Mrs. Burke, we're concerned about Rebecca. She's doing fine in class. Completes her homework on time, but she won't answer questions when she's called on. Is she okay?"

Alarmed, Mom sent her to an ear, nose and throat doctor. Were Rebecca's vocal cords damaged; was she hearing impaired; or was she on the spectrum of autism? Testing revealed her hearing was fine, throat normal and no Asperger diagnosis. The only avenue left would be psychology. Mom had read that a traumatic experience could cause a child to be mute. The slow and expensive therapy didn't reveal a solution. The therapist gently hammered her, "Did someone do something to you, Rebecca? I know it's hard but if you tell me, I can help you. Can you just mouth words?"

Mom's frustrations forced a call to the school principal for answers.

"Rebecca was fine in first grade but as soon as she started second grade, she stopped speaking. Did something happen to her?"

"Let me talk to her first-grade teacher and see if anything happened."

The principal called later that same day, "I spoke to her first-grade teacher, Mrs. Carfango, and she told me that there was an incident with a bully making fun of her lisp. She reprimanded the boy but it's possible he was tormenting her outside of class. Lisping is normal up until first grade, so the teacher wasn't worried about Rebecca."

Edna's fury screamed, "Why wasn't I told about this? Do you know what I've been through trying to get to the root of her muteness? This is unacceptable."

Rebecca's mom had noticed the lisp but remembered when she was a child, she herself had trouble with words ending in "S." Edna's head heard the correct pronunciation while her mouth refused to comply. She outgrew it.

That evening, Edna spoke to Rebecca about the lisp, "Honey, I think I know why you aren't speaking. You're afraid that you'll lisp and that people will make fun of you. It's normal."

Rebecca began crying and threw her petite arms around Edna.

"You'll be fine, Rebecca. How about we get some help? A speech therapist at school will make it disappear. Wouldn't that be great, my darling?"

Rebecca didn't speak but she smiled with the hope that the bullying would end.

Rebecca looked forward to school and during class, a tall crunched-up-faced woman entered the classroom. Mrs. Gerrick announced to Rebecca, "Go with Mrs. Frost, she'll help you with your problem."

Rebecca turned crimson when she left her chair. A few giggles hit her eardrums as she was siphoned out of class. Mrs. Lawson explained, "Just ignore those kids. They are just jealous you get to leave class. We're going to start with flash cards and you'll be fixed in no time."

This logged incident stuck with Rebecca, and she became determined to ease the pain of children with speech disabilities when she attained adulthood. A child shouldn't be embarrassed and made fun of. Mrs. Gerrick's language was inappropriate when she announced to the entire class that Rebecca had a "problem." She should have been reported to the principal.

Chapter 2

Warren in San Diego

Warren's patience was threading. He wanted to apologize even though it wasn't his fault that she got sick. Each angle to ask Rebecca to forgive him failed. Pink Roses delivered to her door and syrupy love letters bombed. Rebecca's apartment was barricaded from him when he drove up from San Diego. She ignored him when he threw pebbles on her window and recreated the scene from the film *Say Anything* where John Cusack holds a boombox in his arms that plays "In Your Eyes" by Peter Gabriel. How could her heart turn to cement? On Thanksgiving, he sat in front of her apartment door waiting for her return. He told his parents he was having dinner with Rebecca's family. They were angry but when they witnessed Warren's drooping bloodshot eyes, they understood his decision. After six hours, hunger devoured his stomach and the setting sun blackened his mood. During the wait, he started biting his nails, a habit that he struggled with for the rest of his life. His cuticles became ragged with blood. His love for Rebecca became a scab getting ripped off daily. His body began rebelling with an outbreak of acne on his chest and back. He resigned himself to writing off Rebecca and stop scratching emotional sores covering his body.

The aching about being separated from Rebecca found a replacement. Warren became fascinated with his own face and stared in the mirror for an hour. His thick beard forced him to shave twice a day to avoid a five o'clock shadow. He traced his hand over his thin eyebrows admiring how they highlighted his deeply etched eyes. His high cheekbones accentuated a masculine bravura. When he checked his nostrils, he realized the oval shape enabled him to scoop up the most secretive odors. The mirror forced him to relinquish Rebecca's hold on him.

His roommate Elijah said, "Hey what are you doing in there? It's been over an hour."

Then the cluttered smelly dorm brought him back to hard-edged reality. Warren barked back, "Just cleaning your shit up. I'll be right out."

Rooming with Elijah had been a tragedy. Elijah ignored Warren's rant, "I don't care that you are a slob on your side of the room. But we share the bathroom. I don't want to see your gook in the sink. And the shower is getting clogged because you don't remove the hair from the drain. And please flush after you pee."

Elijah laughed, "Okay mother. I'll try to do better Mr. Anal." Despite Elijah's insane class load for pre-med that included Chemistry and Biology, his tranquil demeanor came from his incessant pot smoking. He reeked of marijuana and Warren secretly hoped he would inhale the secondhand weed smoke to make him forget about Rebecca.

The culture shock of the military conservative San Diego made Warren careful when mingling with classmates. A discussion about politics would be a lightning rod. Warren wanted to blend. He became a secret liberal. Privately, he'd become a political junkie watching CNN, Fox News if held his nose, and reading the New York Times, New Republic, and Wall Street Journal. During the contested 2000 election between Bush and Gore, Warren was glued to the news. He volunteered for the Gore campaign, canvassing San Diego County. The phone bank calls started with, "Are you registered to vote? I'm working for Al Gore." Followed by hang-ups. On the day that the Supreme Court mandated that the Florida recount end and Bush became the president, Warren vowed to be more vigilant about ensuring that Democrats win future elections. As a future lawyer, he would work to convert non-believers to the Democratic party. No longer in the closet about his political beliefs. He settled on a political science major after considering criminal justice, economics, psychology, and history.

Working twenty hours at Jamba Juice filled up his weekend, leaving no space for dating or socializing with friends unless you counted flirting with customers. Jogging five miles a day was all the nourishment his body needed.

His favorite run was through Balboa Park. Warren enjoyed the freedom of jogging shirtless despite the acne that had ravished his chest and back. He'd worked overtime building muscles and showing them off. The religious experience of smelling his own sweat and being cognizant of his breathing created his own form of spirituality.

The half-way point at The California Tower gave Warren a chance to rest and reengage with the mish-mash of Baroque and Gothic architecture styles on the soaring iconic San Diego building. His refreshed and ready plan to resume jogging abruptly stopped when a scream hit his ears.

A woman dragging her walker was shouting, "Stop him. He stole my purse." Warren spotted the culprit racing off with the woman's bag. A rush to catch the thief resonated through his legs. Warren easily caught the dirty blonde young kid, looking no more than sixteen. Warren grabbed the boy and he dropped the stolen item. Warren didn't release the boy.

He cried, "Let me go."

"No, you can't go around stealing things."

The woman met up with Warren.

"Thank you so much for retrieving this."

Warren responded, "Do you want to report this to the police? Teach this creep a lesson."

"No, that's okay. No harm done."

Warren refused to end the scene.

"What is wrong with you? Stealing an old woman's purse."

The bloodshot eyes, ripped pants, stringy unwashed hair, and dirty fingernails meant the boy was homeless.

"I really should take you to the police despite what that woman said."

He looked down, non-responsive.

Warren said, "Talk to me. Tell me your name."

"Why should I bother? No one gives a fuck about me. It's Philip."

"Philip, shouldn't you be in school? Can I call your parents?"

When he chewed on his filthy fingernails, it reminded Warren of his own nasty habit.

"No. They don't want to hear from me. I ran away from home when I turned eighteen. They hate me."

"What are you talking about?"

"They found out I was gay and their version of grounding me was more like being jailed and then on parole for six months. I was being watched constantly. Practically locked in my bedroom twenty-four/seven. I had to escape."

Warren's homeless guess was correct.

"How are you surviving?"

"I've done some hustling but it's dangerous. If I'm lucky I can spend the night with a guy, otherwise I'm sleeping on the streets."

Both horrified and intrigued by Philip's story, Warren's gut told him that as a future lawyer fighting for LGBT rights could be his calling card.

"Look. Why don't I buy you lunch? And I can help you find a shelter to stay in until we figure out what to do. You've got to be in school."

Warren had found another distraction from obsessing about his first love, Rebecca. Previous methods of wiping the Rebecca slate clean had not worked.

Chapter 3

The Blind Date-4 years later

Rebecca relented after Paul insisted that she meet this unknown man. She hoped a disaster would convince Paul to give up on matchmaking. Brunch at The French Market Place in West Hollywood was the meeting place. The outdoor seating that enjoyed the fumes of Santa Monica Boulevard was offset by eye candy strutting on the sidewalk. Rebecca tried to downplay her prominent features. No makeup, a cap covering her highlighted blonde hair, and a loose tee shirt that left her chest a mystery. Her owl eyes could only be disguised if she wore sunglasses. She would camouflage herself in the gay establishment.

Paul said he'd drive and they'd meet Mr. Anonymous at eleven.

"Paul, are you going to tell me this guy's name?"

"It's a surprise, sister."

She hated surprises, "Oh God a real blind date. This is the last time I'm doing this." Rebecca failed to read Paul's poker face. Their sibling bonding made her trust him implicitly. Rebecca's nerves were on display as they left Paul's Ford Mustang and walked toward the restaurant.

Despite the eighty-degree weather, a cold sweat enveloped her when she saw him. A flight response occurred when she glared at Paul.

"How could you do this? I thought you understood I don't want anything to do with him."

"Come on Rebecca, it's been four years. The statute has run out. At least give Warren a chance. He never got over you."

An electric current rammed at her when Warren rose to greet her. She was cloaked in shallow breaths.

"Oh, Rebecca. You look beautiful. God, I can't believe how much I've been wanting to see you."

Rebecca still wanted to flee but when Warren stared at her without blinking, her shallow breathing returned to normal. He was making love to her with his hazel eyes. She was under his voodoo spell and starved for this man.

Paul backed away and said, "Hey, you guys. I'm gonna split. You have tons to catch up on, and I would just be in the way. Warren, can I trust you to take Rebecca home?"

"You mean I can't kidnap her? Sure, I'll return your dream sister."

Paul checked with Rebecca, "You okay, Rebecca? You'll forgive me for the surprise. You seem happy."

Rebecca hugged Paul and went back to reconnecting with her first and only love. Warren rambled off some of his history. He had moved to Ocean Park in Santa Monica even though Loyola Law School was downtown. His parents had left him a small legacy that he used to pay rent so he could focus on his law classes and exams. He told her, "It's a miniature one-bedroom apartment but a short walk to the beach makes up for a multitude of sins. You'll love the area." Warren's boyish face remained disconnected from his bass voice. When he took Rebecca's hands and said, "You have such exquisite hands. Perfect for a commercial. Nothing like my chewed fingertips from my habit of nail-biting," her body started sexually trembling.

The waiter popped by and was sprouting a name tag, Jeffrey from Kansas City and asked, "What can I get you, kids?"

Warren responded with, "The brunch special and a large Margarita pitcher."

Rebecca said, "I'll have what he's having." Both giggled, sharing their memories of the film *When Harry Met Sally*. In the movie, Meg Ryan explained to Billy Crystal how a woman can fake an orgasm. In the middle of a crowded New York Deli, Meg Ryan proceeded to recreate the orgasm. At the next table, the customer told the waiter, "I'll have what she's having." Rebecca and Warren had watched the film when they met in high school.

"But Warren, how did you reach my brother? Had you ever met my brother before?"

The devilish explanation was, "I ran into him at a fundraiser, Lawyers for Human Rights. He looked familiar. I mean you are brother and sister."

"You never met Paul before? In all that time I was dating you.

Warren snickered, "No, I was your secret love."

"So, you met at this gay organization? Is there something you want to tell me?"

Warren laughed while Rebecca continued, "There was a notice at the community board at Loyola. I asked around and my study partner Melvin said he'd been volunteering for the organization. Melvin said one of the organizers, David Mixner, was up for an award. Mixner was sort of a legend as an anti-war activist in the 1960s and gay rights advocate."

"Were you the only straight man there?"

"Maybe. I wanted to start networking while I was going to law school. I'd gotten interested in gay rights. Anyway, I started chatting with your brother and when I told him my name, he said that I'd really done a number on his sister. I tried to explain what happened. He said you were lonely and never dated."

"I'll kill him. He feels like he has to protect me. It's none of his business. He thinks I've hired him as my matchmaker"

"But look at how it's turned out."

Warren took hold of her face, gazing at each feature. Her mile-long eyelashes and sun-bleached hair were launching pads making her a divine presence.

"I'm sorry I shut you out but I was so devastated about herpes. I was convinced you'd infected me. When I questioned the doctor, she decided to do some additional testing. Turns out I had a mild case of a depressed immune system and this left me open to opportunistic infections like herpes. Luckily it wasn't Epstein Barr."

"And I'm just as much at fault, Rebecca. I was an idiot, and I stopped calling you. Gave up coming to Los Angeles. I was a real ass. Are you okay health-wise?"

"Yes, I'm fine. The doctor monitors my blood and I have to watch that I don't get run down. You know the usual, eight hours of sleep and eating healthy."

The four years of separation dissolved when they had makeup sex. And to give some levity to the enormity of the reunion, Warren started a ritual of tickling her feet. For the rest of their lives, the power of laughter glued them together. Inevitably they were both on track to marry after Warren passed the bar. Rebecca quickly squeezed into Warren's apartment, finished her degree and began doing speech therapy at the Pearl Street grade school. Warren passed the bar on his first try and slowly started his sole civil litigation practice in an office on Beverly Drive and Olympic. With a Beverly Hills address, he hoped he could attract high-end clients for his auto accidents, slip and falls cases along with medical malpractice. His fighting for gay rights was sidelined.

Paul was an instrumental part of their lives. Rebecca and Paul had never lived apart until she wrapped herself into Warren's life. Paul held onto the Silverlake abode by enlisting a revolving door of roommates. Rebecca worried about him not settling down because he had a parade of men he dated. His acting career had faltered and attaining a teaching position had eluded him. She insisted that Paul be included in dinner plans weekly.

Chapter 4
Gay and Acting

Paul was born in 1983 a year after his sister's birth. He couldn't remember a time when he was clueless about being gay. His attraction to men was spiritual. The gods were shining on him because he was living in the enclave that would soon become West Hollywood. In seventh grade at Bancroft Junior High, he had his first encounter. He spotted an unfamiliar boy running track after school. His muscular legs and arms were in stark contrast to Paul's emaciated frame. He had that senior-junior high look about him. Paul fantasized that he took off his sweaty white tee-shirt.

"You were really pushing it out there. What's your time for a mile?"

As his toothy smile filled his face, the boy said, "I don't check it. I'm trying to build endurance."

"Hey, do you want to hang out? I found this really cool house. It's sort of a secret hiding place."

"Can you give me about fifteen minutes? I need to shower. I must stink."

Paul inhaled the masculine odor and the heat emanating from his body. He followed the boy to the showers telling him, "I need to take a piss."

The showers were deserted. Paul couldn't stop staring when his first promising catch stripped and adjusted the shower temperature. The art of the male physique fascinated Paul as his compatriot soaped up.

The boy didn't flinch. He liked being watched. Paul wanted to keep ogling at the stranger's puppy dog eyes. The wet curly hair framed his boy-man face as they walked out of campus.

"So where is this place you're taking me to?"

"An abandoned house on Formosa near Melrose. I found a break in the fence that surrounds the property that we can crawl under."

He said, "I haven't seen you in class."

"I just finished seventh grade."

"Oh yeah. I'm a senior. Going to Fairfax when I graduate." This revelation crushed Paul's attraction.

"I plan to attend Hollywood High. I want to be an actor. I know you're thinking I'm so short. How can I be a star?"

"No, aren't you still growing? Look at Tom Cruise and Dustin Hoffman."

"Both my parents were short so I don't have much hope to grow."

At the house, Paul attempted to drag his new buddy through the dilapidated fence entrance. The daylight prevented the overgrown dandelions, burnt grass and peeling yellow paint from giving the place Haunted House status. His novel friend had a puzzled look, "Are you sure we can fit through?"

Paul realized that size mattered.

"Let's see if we can pull the fence apart so you can fit."

Once that task was complete, they both crawled through the opening trying to ignore the enveloping dirt. The juice strainer exercise came to a halt when a ripping sound was audible. Paul said, "Come on. Let me help you squeeze through before you tear anymore of your pants."

After they righted themselves, Paul dusted the soot off both of them.

Paul said, "Hey it looks like you scratched your arm. There is blood. Are you okay?"

"I'm fine. I can call it a badge of honor when I tell the guys about my encounter with a fence. I'll tell them I was breaking and entering." Paul dreamed of possessing him.

They entered through the open back door and tiptoed through the gutted kitchen area. A small area packed off in the corner was a resting stop.

Sun filtered through the room bouncing off a poster of *Star Wars*. Paul prayed for assistance from "The Force" to complete the afternoon delight. He asked, "Have you ever wrestled?"

That was the trigger. Angel boy gripped Paul. Elbows were smashed against the floor with growling eyes eating away at Paul. Paul had little strength to overtake him but used a distraction technique to throw off his aggressor. He used his trunk to wiggle away. With his arms free he started to hug the man. Paul's hormones were working overtime. The goal of kissing came next but when their lips were within inches, a scuttering noise stopped their physical embrace. Paul screamed when he saw the large tail of a rat running into the kitchen. They both jumped up screaming. The screams turned to giggles.

"Scared of a little rat."

Paul replied, "You screamed too."

"We better get out of here. Who knows what else is lurking around? Let's race back to Bancroft. That's near my house."

A sour candy ending to Paul's anti-climactic adventure.

With Paul's short legs he couldn't keep up. His angel seemed oblivious to Paul's breathless race that turned into a slow jog. Paul vowed to never let an encounter like that slip by.

When he turned sixteen and started Hollywood High, Paul conquered football, baseball and the ridiculous challenge of basketball. To make up for his stunted five-foot-eight size, he became obsessed with building muscle. His hard-edged piercing blue-green eyes contrasted with his smile made him unconquerable. His hairy chest formed the design of a cross that complemented the bristling hair covering his legs.

He wasn't ashamed about his allure to boys, but he didn't flaunt his gayness. He passed as a straight white boy in high school but when he was questioned, "Paul aren't there any girls you're interested in? Whom are you taking to the prom? Have you had sex yet?" he refused to lie. Paul either ignored the queries or changed the subject.

Beginning in eleventh grade his quest to nail the lead in plays shot to the top of his bucket list. Paul was a double threat combining athletic triumphs and theatrical expertise. Paul knew it was easier to attain his status at Hollywood High compared to super competitive Fairfax High.

Paul auditioned for the part of Willy Loman in *Death of a Salesman*. Playing a man forty years older than Paul who loses his identity and his inability to accept change within himself and society, was challenging. Paul spent hours transforming physical traits to mirror a fifty-five-year-old defeated man.

He used his smallness to his advantage. Movements mirrored a geriatric gait. He assimilated world-weariness in his eyes building to the scene where Willy confesses, "After all the highways, and the trains, and the appointments, and the years, you end up worth more dead than alive." Paul struggled to make that line ring out. After doing an all-nighter before the audition, he was ready.

Mr. Aaron was doing the casting and ushered Paul to the barren stage. Paul morphed into Willy and gingerly walked to the brightly lit space. Mr. Aaron along with a team of assistants didn't smile during Paul's monologue. Paul had drilled into Willy, ignoring the fate of the audition. Professor Aaron thanked Paul. The casting choices would be announced the following week.

Paul's cocky personality got him through the tumultuous seven day wait. The proclamation was posted outside Mr. Aaron's classroom. Paul waited until his taller competitors checked for their name, mostly leaving in defeat. Paul gasped and squealed like a baby. Paul Burke-Willy Loman. Opening night set the stage for Paul's launching pad to acting.

Paul smiled remembering his Bancroft friends who were confused by his Hollywood High School choice and told him, "I can't believe you won't be going to Fairfax. Don't you want to try at least one semester? You're crazy to go to Hollywood High."

"I like being different and I'm going to seize the opportunity."

They would be regurgitating their words after his Hollywood High accomplishments. Paul surpassed Mr. Popular status and he filled up his extra-curricular activities fulfilling acting pursuits. He went to Stella Adler's acting classes. Stella was part of the Group Method invented by Konstantin Stanislavski. The Method nurtured actors to use their imagination. De Niro and Brando were the highest-profiled results from this technique. Even though Stella had died in 1992, her legacy lived on with the school on Hollywood Boulevard a few blocks east of Grauman's Chinese Theater, home of celebrity footprints. Paul loved the idea of living inside characters that he portrayed even when he wasn't in acting class or on stage.

Paul auditioned at the Callboard, Cast, Zephyr, and Matrix. All ninety-nine seat equity waiver theaters where Paul didn't need to be a member of the Actor's union. Even with the fierce competition outside of the school bubble, Paul had no regrets. The only wrinkle were Paul's sexual activities that had started to threaten his success after graduation.

Paul's birth coincided with the explosion of the AIDS plague. Sexual education included safe sex mandates where the use of a condom was required. He made it a point to ask the HIV status of partners, and if they were positive, he reframed from anal intercourse and oral sex. Besides, he had no frame of reference to the sexual freedoms of the 1970s. A world of safe sex was all he knew. Still, he had multiple conquests of boys at Hollywood High. Most were closeted but because Paul appeared straight, he was a safe choice.

And being a West Hollywood resident gave Paul access to young guys his age. He was underage, so bars were off limits unless he got a fake I.D. Even with an I.D., his height made him look like a child. The rap groups at The Gay and Lesbian Community Center were another venue for tricking. When they did a round robin of questions at the raps, the responses didn't resonate with Paul; "I'm so lonely. I hate being gay. I'm always getting bullied." His sister had been a saint when he came out to her. She wasn't surprised and said, "I figured you were gay. You never once mentioned crushes on girls. And you are such a fashion person. You always look perfect."

The move to Silverlake in 2004 with his sister, brought him new pursuits. No longer competing with the plastic boy models of Weho, the rougher more authentic gay men in Silverlake were easier to capture. No bullshit. He had a gigantic pool to choose from. Paul kept a list and his goal of one hundred prized men before he finished his 21st year, was reachable.

His Saturday night ritual began with the Blue-plate special at Eat Well on Sunset Boulevard. The comfort food of roast beef and buttered mashed potatoes filled his stomach to the brim. Next stop was The Faultline, the premier leather bar near the cross section of Sunset Boulevard (Route 66) and Fountain. Route 66 was The Main Street of America or the Mother Road, the first major American Highway established in 1926. Sunset Boulevard covers the part of Route 66 that starts at Olvera Street in Downtown Los Angeles and ends at the Pacific Ocean.

Working the Faultline room came naturally to Paul. The bottom button of his 501 jeans was left open, and the required bulky leather jacket completed Paul's costume. Flirting with the half-naked bartenders while slurping Corona was an attention grabber. Dancing to Janet Jackson's "What Have You Done for me Lately?" let Paul's feet fly. If the action was substandard, he moved to Cuffs on Hyperion at the stroke of midnight. The smoke-filled dimly lit bar, filled with bears enticed Paul. Bears were pot-bellied and bearded gay men with pussycat personalities. Paul had no type or age restrictions, except for eyes. Paul followed the mantra *Eyes are the window to your soul* when he chose the man of the night.

The witching hour of two a.m. closing time ushered him to capture his game. The only blonde in the pack named Stephen winked at Paul signaling him to follow. The fresh air entered Paul's lungs after two hours of cigarette perfume. His leather jacket would be ruined and need an intense cleaning. Stephen grabbed his hand. His ocean blues contrasted with his chubby frame. A half-moon partially exposed his face.

"Where's your car? Did you want to follow me back to my place?"

"Is it far?"

Stephen said, "No, about half a mile. My ankle has been bothering me and I usually drive."

"I'll come with you and just walk back to my car in the morning."

The steep Silverlake hills created fifty steps to get to Stephen's apartment after parking. After entering the apartment Stephen asked, "Want anything to drink, Paul?"

"Water is fine."

"I would show you around but it's a studio, this is it, one big room." Stephen made the place look expansive because of his space organization skills. The functional kitchen area was spotless. The black and white photographic prints of Robert Mapplethorpe and Herb Ritts filled the walls.

While Paul slurped water, he told Stephen, "Don't get offended. I need to ask if you are HIV positive. I'm very active and want to be careful."

"I get it. I get tested once a year and always get negative results." The kissing commenced and the freeform evening of sexual exercise lasted until early morning. Paul had a rule about not spending the night and explained, "Stephen I'm going to walk back to my car before the sun comes up. Thank you for tonight."

Stephen wanted to sleep with Paul, wake up in the morning together, and have breakfast at The Crest coffee shop. He frowned at the prospect of being deserted.

"Paul, it's four in the morning. Why don't you stay?"

"No, I have to go. Sorry." A final kiss and Paul was back on the street to find his blue Mustang. The smelly leather jacket fortified Paul from the chilly morning. When the car was within his sightline, he noticed a few boys pacing on the sidewalk. Paul nonchalantly continued walking towards his car.

"Hey, faggot. What are you doing here?"

Paul tried to ignore them. He pulled out his car keys from his tight jeans and the second the key entered the door; the larger boy grabbed hold of him and he was thrown to the ground. Paul shouted, "Help!"

"We don't want any queers in this neighborhood."

Kicks to his stomach stopped Paul from getting up from the sidewalk. The deadly quiet neighborhood ignored his screams. His organs shrieked in fear of demolition with each bludgeon. An explosive shot rang through the street, and Paul let terror ripple through him. He'd heard about gang drive-by shootings, worrying about that sequence of events while he lay paralyzed on the ground. The boys scattered and an energy burst allowed Paul to roll towards his Mustang to safety from the rumbling Thunderbird scorching the street. The sputtering exhaust pipe coming from the car was responsible for what Paul thought was a gunshot. Paul sighed in relief. After enabling himself to stand up and check for body damage, he took deep breaths to slow his racing muscles.

He keeled over from the pain emanating from his stomach and surrounding organs. The Eat Well dinner exploded from his esophagus. He robotically entered his car and tried to focus on driving home where showering and crawling into bed would heal his wounds. Luckily, the leather jacket had protected his elbows from scraping when he hit the ground. Paul didn't believe in God but he needed someone to thank for saving him from the violent abyss that had ended his innocence.

Thank you, mother earth.

The slow out-of-body driving experience back to his apartment let Paul block out the trauma he'd suffered.

He prayed that Rebecca was asleep so he wouldn't have to confront her with the gay bashing. She'd been known to be on the couch reading Anne Tyler or snoozing when he dragged himself in from his latest escapade. His older sister loved mothering her twenty-one-year-old baby brother since Mom had mild cognitive impairment. Edna had always been forgetful, but recently she tried to use a clothes iron to dry her hair and her bathtub had overflowed because she forgot to turn off the faucet. He wanted to believe the thirty-mile away Beach Woods community, where she had moved, would stave off a fully blown Alzheimer's diagnosis for his mother Edna.

Paul stripped and looked at his abdomen for bruising. The discolored areas were tender but the spasms and nausea had stopped. He hoped that the workout regimen that resulted in washboard abs was a defense against any internal damage.

The beating shower cleared his head and he collapsed onto his bed, instantly falling into a deep slumber. No Sunday commitments. He had twenty-four hours to recuperate before Monday classes. Paul's career goals encapsulated the entire theatrical spectrum. Standup comedy, improv, playwriting, kitchen sink dramas, and if all that collapsed becoming a drama teacher. The Cal State Northridge classes grounded him.

Sunday morning, Paul walked quietly into the partially covered pool area. The reflecting light rippled through the smell of the heavily chlorinated water. Blue walls were bleeding into the crackled pool tiles. The temperate water eased the dive into the pool. Spigots of water spit on his arms. After the body announced that thirty laps were sufficient, the heavy-duty Israeli cotton towel dried him off. The adjacent jacuzzi bubbled after turning the knob that brought the jets to life. The almost scalding hot water soothed stomach bruises. Dunking his head in the chlorinated water was the final baptism before ejecting himself. Sitting on the peeling bench by the pool and letting droplets fall to the ground as he read Michael Cunningham's *A Home at The End of the World* gave him ammunition to face the remainder of the day. He was rejuvenated, dried fruit waiting to be picked by another handsome stranger. But he would be more vigilant and get involved with politics of gay rights, starting at the LGBT center.

Chapter 5
Marriage

In early 2005, Rebecca introduced Warren to the restaurant Il Forno on Ocean Park Boulevard which was a short walk from the school Rebecca was teaching at. Il Forno was the go-to restaurant where co-workers would celebrate birthdays. When they approached the restaurant, smells of Italian spices made their stomachs growl. After entering the establishment, Rebecca asked for a special waiter while Warren admired the interior that sported large windows that opened to a patio shrouded with trees.

After they situated themselves, Ernesto, their waiter carrying a tray, told them, "Hi. Rebecca asked me to make something special since it's your first time, Warren."

The tray had two small plates filled with rolled eggplant stuffed with goat cheese herbs and tomato sauce and a third miniature covered plate.

Ernesto proceeded to place the melanzane in front of Rebecca and Warren and the petite plate by Warren.

"What's this?"

"It's a surprise. Just lift the cover. It's not going to bite you," Rebecca said.

Warren slowly took the cover off and smiled when his eyes focused on the contents.

Rebecca tearfully asked, "Would you be my husband, Mr. Warren Knight?"

She took the wedding band and slipped it on Warren's finger before he could answer.

"Yes Rebecca, only if you'll become my wife."

Rebecca and Warren married at the architectural landmark on Pacific Coast Highway, the beach house of Marion Davies. William Randolph Hearst had built the home for his wife, Marion, by one of the first California female architects, Julia Morgan. Rebecca's friend Jackie played the role of the wedding planner, and during the event, she supervised the caterers. Jackie had removed all the stress from the wedding for Warren and Rebecca. The sea air hypnotized the participants while they stood on the wood planks across the patio. A lingering insecurity about his looks hadn't been a hundred percent conquered. Once Warren had reunited with Rebecca, he retired his neurotic obsession with his face. He no longer spent nervous hours facing the mirror looking for his own imperfections. Still, the lingering nail-biting remained an unchecked habit. Gratefully, Rebecca's amazon stride of fearlessness took Warren into a joyous space.

The ceremony began when the sun was crashing into the ocean. Brick red clouds filled the sky while Warren and Rebecca vowed to each other. Lacking any strong religious beliefs, Robert, a judge friend of Warren, officiated the proceedings. Rebecca crowned the event with her off-white dress and the face of the Greek goddess, Aphrodite, eternally young with boundless beauty. Rebecca was proud to wear no makeup

The wedding party included Edna, Uncle Buddy, lawyers from Warren's office, Jackie and the band of teachers from Rebecca's Pearl Street School. Cousins of Warren and his northern California uncle and aunt made up the remaining family invitees. Warren's parents never got to meet Rebecca. After both recovered from cancer, they died in a head-on collision five years before, an impetus for him to become a civil litigation lawyer. Rebecca's cousins on her father's side were scattered across the country and couldn't make the affair. Whole Foods catered the buffet that stretched across the walls of the house. Vegan and vegetarian guests were easily accommodated.

Rebecca had told Warren during the wedding planning stages, "I'd like Paul to be your best man and give the toast." Warren worshiped Rebecca and granted her wishes.

Paul graced the group with his speech about their closeness as brother and sister and ended with, "I'm not losing a sister, I am gaining a brother."

Paul couldn't stop staring at Warren. He'd recently acquired an insane crush on Warren that confused him. Had Warren put a spell on Rebecca that somehow included him? There was a mysterious familiarity with Warren that remained unsolved. Did they meet at the Diamond Fitness gym? Paul didn't believe it was déjà vu. He knew they had met. An unfastened memory gashed Paul. The runner encountered at Bancroft Junior High. Watching Warren shower and the field trip to the haunted house on Formosa. Then the moment of sexual reckoning was sabotaged by a stupid rat. Apparently, Warren didn't let on that he remembered the event and Paul wouldn't bring it up. And they never did anything really. This was not the kind of information Rebecca should be made aware of.

Rebecca couldn't hold back her emotions when Paul spoke. She worried their relationship would be tested despite Paul's insistence that he didn't feel abandoned when she moved in with Warren. She worried that Warren's sweet acceptance of Paul as a third party would stretch his patience.

Warren cringed during the speech, worried that the brother-sister bond was bordering on unhealthy. After Paul spoke,

"In Whatever Time We Have" echoed through the hall. He questioned Rebecca why she chose the song from the obscure musical *Children of Eden* written by the composer of *Wicked*, Stephen Schwartz. The lyrics bordered on morbid with the suggestion that the end of the world was coming but the lovers would have each other until then. Rebecca said she loved the sentiment and Warren knew this wasn't a hill worth dying on. Warren seized Rebecca for the first dance.

In the evening Warren had reserved a room at the Elizabeth Bed and Breakfast in Malibu within walking distance of the beach. Warren carried Rebecca across the threshold of the room. Warren told her, "Did you know this tradition came from "The Rape of Sabine Women" in Roman mythology?"

"That sounds awful. Put me down. It's kidnapping!"

"No, my love. It's been reinterpreted that the bride doesn't want to seem too eager to leave her parents so the husband transports his love through the door."

A lilac smell rolled through the suite. The king-size four-poster bed canopy sweetened their first night as husband and wife. Warren and Rebecca splashed their congratulation cards across the mattress and read them out loud. Humbled by the honey-laced day, they slumbered until their exhaustion passed. Warren continued his practice of tickling Rebecca's feet. Her giggling launched his own laughter when she reciprocated with her own tickling of Warren's underarms. Both were lost in the physicality of the comic connection.

Once revived, their conversation volleyed between their past, present and future.

"You know when I was a little girl, I never dreamed about getting married. I didn't want a white knight to sweep me off my feet. I wasn't interested in being taken care of or taking care of someone. So, when I met you in high school, I never thought we'd marry. Of course, I fought against this insane crush."

"You just liked me because I looked like a mashup of Ben Affleck and John Cusack. So that's why you seduced me like Mrs. Robinson in *The Graduate* when you announced that I could make love to you."

She kissed Warren when she exclaimed, "Oh God, yes. I knew what I wanted sexually. And Mrs. Robinson was an older woman. Wrong reference, Warren!"

Warren shot back, "You were little Miss Independent!"

"So, I never needed to understand why I fell in love with you. There was no list of positive and negative traits. When you held me in your arms, when we talked, and when we looked at each other, we were in a magic zone. I had no other thoughts. Like when I do my mindful meditation. We are on the same energy wavelength."

Warren was overwhelmed and his eyes and ears sent Morse codes to his brain. Tapping love into Warren's soul.

"Rebecca, you make it so easy to love you. I was always afraid to let someone love me. That it would be taken away."

Rebecca smiled, "Enough with this sentimentality. I want to tell you what happened at school last week. One of my problematic students, Ken, had his parents show up unannounced when I was doing therapy. Plus, they wanted to videotape the session. I was freaked out but after ten minutes, I just ignored them. And you know, there was a breakthrough with their son. I saw his face and his parents light up when he communicated. The first time he said the words Papa and Momma. I caught myself weeping at Ken's accomplishment."

"You are extraordinarily patient and devoted. And you have helped me so much with my cases. You bring a fresh point of view. When I talk to you, it clears my head."

"You do ramble when describing what happens with clients, but I love the sound of your voice. And of course, always referring to them as clients for confidentiality. Your passion for the law makes me love you."

Rebecca deserved more than a kiss but playtime would come later in the evening.

"It's hard for me to keep track of all the lawyer lingo, Abacus Brief, mediation, statutes and discovery."

"But you are amazing, my beautiful wife. And guess what? The case against Elaine Rich Community Hospital (ERCH) is huge. And when I was getting hot-headed, you calmed me down as to how to deal with them. And suggesting that I ask the other lawyers in the office what ERCH usually settles for was brilliant. I think we'll have enough for a small down payment in Ocean Garden."

"You mean that complex on Pearl and Twenty-first? Oh God, I could walk to work. And it would be a perfect place to raise children. Wouldn't it be amazing if I got pregnant tonight?"

"Let's not get too ahead of ourselves. We've been married less than twenty-four hours. Don't we want to get to really know each other before we add to our family?"

They giggled thinking they knew everything about each other:

Favorite color: he-aqua blue, she-purple

Favorite film: he-*Chinatown*, she-*E.T.*

Favorite food: he-Italian, she-Thai

Favorite book: he-*To Kill a Mockingbird*, she-*Diary of Anne Frank*

The timing of children remained a question mark. Rebecca and Warren frequently spoke about how many children they wanted. Warren envisioned baby-making in the distant future.

He vacillated about children. Financial security had to come first, and he wasn't on board with sharing this information with Rebecca on their honeymoon. He'd recently witnessed his obese lawyer friend Larry's catch-22 on the subject.

During lunch at Factor's Deli within walking distance of their office, Larry told him, "Be careful before you decide to have kids. I know you love Rebecca and you would never think about breaking up, but you never know. Having children changes the dynamics."

"But I want to make Rebecca happy. I think I'd be a good father. Isn't that what marriage is all about?"

The waitresses interrupted with a half sandwich piled sky high with *corned* beef for Warren and a full pastrami for insatiable Larry.

"Yes, but Rebecca is young. Her biological clock has plenty of time. I'm just saying don't rush it."

Warren stuck the children issue deep into his brain procrastinating any further discussion with Rebecca.

Rebecca and Warren's first night of matrimony continued with the sound of the summer waves that enticed them to walk to the beach. The crystalized night showered stars that Warren recognized.

"The Big Dipper is beautiful tonight. And look at the moon. Each crater is visible." They let their hugging body warmth suppress the chilly September night as they removed their shoes and dug their feet into the sand.

Rebecca shivered, "I'm cold, husband."

"No, let me rub your fingers and create a hotspot."

"Honey, we really need to get back. I know my body and I'm shaking from the cold."

Warren was her obedient servant as they pranced back to their suite. Sharing a shower and scrubbing each other's bodies in the midst of tickling defrosted the love birds. The heavy embroidered midnight blue towels invigorated their skin. Before their erotic sleep, they formed an unspoken pact that making love nightly was their soul nourishment. Their first twenty-four hours of marriage came to a grand finale.

Chapter 6
Edna

Edna's first five years at Beach Woods had given her renewed brain functioning. Even though Beach Woods had decayed from its fresh virgin status when it opened in 1962, it had enough positive elements to outweigh the rundown atmosphere. The Torrance location gave the residents an abundance of life-enhancing negative ions from the ocean breeze. Round-the-clock nurses, physicians, and outpatient medical services were available within the senior community. The daily engaging activities consisted of bingo, barbecues, drawing classes, chair yoga, trivia contests and meditation for seniors. The biggest drawback came from the military compound within shouting distance of the complex. It was home to nightly loud explosions that rattled the sanity of residents. Edna's impaired hearing saved her from that auditory assault.

She shared a two-bedroom unit with eighty-five-year-old ornery Glenda and they bonded instantly. Both were addicted to the soap opera *Days of Our Lives* and bridge. Glenda and Edna hated cooking but together they were able to patch together simple recipes of baked chicken, turkey loaf, and salmon croquettes.

Still, Edna's faculties began descending in January 2006 and her short-term memory vanished. When Rebecca and Paul visited, she got confused about who they were. Edna's brain raced to dementia.

In the dog days of summer, Glenda called the front desk, "My roommate, Edna, is missing. We both went to sleep at nine and when I got up this morning, she wasn't in her room. We always have breakfast together."

The sprawling complex covering 542 park-like acres divided into spaces called Mutuals challenged the staff to find Edna among the nine thousand residents. The three guarded gate entrances used to prevent uninvited guests wouldn't prevent occupants from escaping.

The administrative staff headed by Arthur Jackson held off contacting Rebecca and Paul until the search party had exhausted the initial twenty-four-hour hunt for Edna. The vigilant pursuit came up blank by nightfall. The local police were notified with a description of Edna.

The silver alert blasted, *looking for a seventy-year-old woman, confused, reddish hair, five foot three.*

At nine in downtown Torrance, Edna sat on the local minibus "A" stop bench. The unencumbered two and half-mile walk took Edna most of the day to complete. The police spotted Edna smiling, realized she fit the missing person's description and returned her to Beach Woods. When the policeman assisted Edna into the police car she said, "Oh Paul. Thank you for taking me home. I wondered where you were?"

Upon arrival back at Beach Woods, Mr. Jackson escorted Edna to her apartment to gather her belongings.

Glenda launched into tears, seeing the return of Edna.

"I was so worried about you. Where did you go, Edna?"

"I was a naughty girl."

The muddled look on Edna's face after Glenda hugged her, spelled out her further deterioration. Mr. Jackson told Glenda,

"We're going to hold her in the Outpatient Health Center but wanted to give you a chance to say goodbye. I know how close you've been."

Glenda told her friend, "Now you be good. You have a lovely daughter and son. They'll take good care of you." Edna kept silently smiling.

Rebecca and Paul were notified by Mr. Jackson and told that Edna needed a memory care unit. Because she had escaped and considered a danger to herself, she would require hospitalization immediately. Beach Woods couldn't be held responsible.

The startling phone call came through just as light sleeper Rebecca had drifted off. Dead to the world, Warren continued his REM or rapid eye movement slumber. She nudged him awake, "Mom was found miles away from the facility and now they want her moved to a nursing home that handles severe dementia patients. I can't understand how quickly she's gone downhill. I just saw her last week and she appeared okay."

"I can't believe they are calling you in the middle of the night to move her. That's bullshit. It's a copout because they don't want to get sued."

"I'm going to call Paul, get dressed and drive down to Torrance."

"Do you want me to come, Rebecca?"

"No, I can do it, and Paul will be with me to figure out where she can go."

She kissed him after he said, "I love you, Rebecca."

Rebecca threw on sweatpants, grabbed her oversized handbag, and called Paul. There was no answer. She'd begged him to leave his phone on in case there was an emergency with Mom. She'd kill him if he was out tricking again. He promised he would stop. His constant sexual prowess was dangerous and unhealthy.

After another failed iPhone attempt while driving to his apartment in Silverlake, she considered driving to Beach Woods herself. Her plummeting exhaustion would make the drive treacherous. Damn Paul. She tried to pry her eyes open before she continued until the *beacon* ring tone sound came through.

"Hey Rebecca, what's going on? Don't you teach tomorrow? This is way past your bedtime."

"I'm coming to pick you up. We're going to get Mom. She wandered off the grounds today. Full-blown dementia, and we've got to get her in a nursing home or hospitalize her tonight. They are holding her."

'Shit. Okay just let me know when you get to the apartment and I'll come down."

"Bring coffee. I'm sleepy. I'm not going to ask where you've been for the last hour. I don't want to know. I'm just glad you picked up and called me."

Ten minutes later, Paul jumped into Rebecca's Accord. The caffeine fix perked up Rebecca while she slurped from the mug Paul gave her.

"I needed this."

"Yes, the wonders of having a Keurig."

During the drive, Paul shared the news about his career with Rebecca, "I've been auditioning all over town. I don't want to jinx it, but I'm this close to getting the second lead in *Glass Menagerie* at The Noise Within. That's the theater in Glendale that only does revivals."

Since Paul had graduated from Cal State Northridge, auditioning had become a ritual. The odds were against him. His height limited parts he could try out for. Still, the lashing of his ego from rejections didn't faze him.

Rebecca wasn't in the mood for Paul's star-struck dreams, "Paul, can you start looking up places that have memory care so we have some ideas as to where we can place Mom?"

When the car landed in Torrance, Rebecca said, "Let me handle things with the director and you stay with Mom. I don't know what kind of condition she is in." Exiting the car, they clung to each other walking into the office. The calming deep breaths of the sea air temporarily calmed their anxiety.

Edna smiled when they entered. The threesome hug mixed with tears lingered until Edna said, "Oh, Sarah and Ed, I'm so glad you came to get me. I've been waiting all day for you."

Sarah and Ed were Edna's parents. Rebecca had little recollection of her grandparents who died before Rebecca became a teenager. Rebecca's guts exploded and she needed to relieve herself in the bathroom before continuing. Paul's stomach roared, realizing the depths of Edna's descent into dementia hell. Paul stayed with Edna while Rebecca talked to the physician. The outpatient center informed her that their mom had a severe UTI, a urinary tract infection, which exaggerated her dementia. Hospital admission was suggested at Long Beach United. Despite the poverty-stricken section of downtown Long Beach, the speed of admission and kindness of the staff bolstered sister and brother. Once Edna was tucked into her new space at the hospital, Rebecca and Paul were able to leave temporarily guilt-free.

The endless night brought sister and brother an avalanche of fucked up emotions. The wee hours of the morning were upon them when they returned to Silverlake and Santa Monica. Rebecca left a message with her school boss about a sick day request and nourished her body with sleep. She had the ability to shut down the noise in her head while Paul's brain refused to let him sleep. He worried that responsibility for Edna would fall on him because he wasn't in a relationship and didn't have a full-time job.

During Edna's stay, underlying conditions were discovered. A CAT Scan revealed a suspicious mass on her kidney resulting in further testing. The diagnosis of stage four cancer came within two days. The consultation with the doctor led to hospice care because Edna became incapable of eating. Her brain waves were shutting down. Uncle Buddy volunteered to have Edna on hospice care in his apartment. Warren put his career on hold, cutting his workaholic hours to eight hours a day and Rebecca took a leave of absence from teaching. They provided twenty-four-hour care, helping Edna with bathing, brushing her teeth, dressing her and towards her demise, assistance with her toilet functions. The hospice nurse handled pain management for the cancer. A week before Edna died, Rebecca received a call,

"Hello, is this Edna?"

"No, this is her daughter."

"Can I speak to her? I'm David. I try to call Edna a few times a year. When I called last week, her friend, Glenda, at Beach Woods gave me this number."

"Oh, I remember Mom talking about you. Something to do with the Chris Brownlie Hospice Facility. Were you another nurse?"

"No, I actually was a patient. I'm a long-term AIDS survivor. Edna took care of me. My lover had died and I'd given up. Letting the virus kill me. Edna counseled me. She said she'd looked at my viral load and that there was a chance with the new cocktail that I had a chance."

"Yes, Edna mentioned how special you were to her."

David visited Edna the following day. David's appearance soothed Rebecca and Warren when his soulful eyes unflinchingly stared at them. He was a shaman who came to heal Edna. Her blank mind went into overdrive when she saw his face.

"David, how are you?"

"Good. I'm a walking miracle because of you. I wanted to thank you for saving my life."

Paul and Rebecca glowed, listening to the spark of lucidity Mom was encountering. "It was my job, David."

David kissed Edna, sat beside her bed, and began massaging her fingers.

"David, did you say hello to my husband, Michael? He's been taking good care of me." David understood the dementia confusion. He had become a nurse in the memory care unit at Saint Mitchell's.

Edna squirmed because she'd been unable to cry out. Her dried lips were glued together, so Rebecca brought water to Edna's lips. Edna beamed with pride. This might be the last expression of love and gratitude for her daughter. The automatic morphine pump kicked in and Edna delved into sleep.

David knew the signs of transitioning but held back telling her children.

"Keep me posted about Edna. I would like to see her again."

Buddy, Rebecca, Warren and Paul were with Edna when she died in June 2007. Without saying the words, the three agreed that death would be better than being mentally incapacitated and unable to take care of herself.

The speed at which Edna died left Rebecca and Paul in a numb and shocked state. Becoming orphans encouraged their closeness. Both became incompetent mourners. No six stages of grief for them. Each nourished their loss with gimmicks of distractions. They consolidated their pity with, "We're not going to start crying, or it will never stop."

Surprisingly, Warren easily expressed his grief during the private memorial service at Buddy's apartment, "It's a cliché to say Edna was the best mother-in-law in the world. I called her mom from the moment I met her. My wife absorbed the unrestricted love that was the lifeblood of Edna's life as a nurse. I won't just miss Edna. I will follow her example of unconditional support with my law practice clients." Warren collapsed weeping into Rebecca's lap after his tribute to Edna. Edna's affection surpassed that of his aloof parents. Edna wanted cremation and her ashes were scattered into Silverlake at the end of the memorial.

During the months after Edna's death, Warren worried about Rebecca converting to a workaholic and Paul taking his sexual addiction to further dangerous territory. He prayed that a healthy dose of grief would catch up with them before they punished themselves with high-octane regrets.

Since Edna's Alzheimer's diagnosis, Edna's portfolio had been handled by Rebecca to enable Mom to live comfortably. A mixture of bonds and certificates of deposit threw off enough monthly income to cover expenses and leave the principal intact. These conservative investments were inherited equally by Paul and Rebecca.

At the tail end of 2007, Rebecca told Paul, "I think you should invest your inheritance in this partnership. Susan, another teacher, told me they are getting eight percent interest. You normally can't get anything close to that. If you invested your entire share of $300,000, it would generate close to $2,000 a month."

"That would be great to fall back on while I get my acting career going. I do okay working at Italian Home Kitchen, but the tips are inconsistent. Is the investment safe?"

"I'll find out from my friends at school and get the paperwork set up."

"Are you investing in the funds too?"

"Yes, but I want to use most of it on the down payment for the townhouse in Ocean Garden."

Chapter 7
The Move

As a teenager, each weekend found Warren at Santa Monica Beach. He spent an hour on the Wilshire Bus from his family's apartment on Kingsley Drive in Mid-Wilshire. His involvement in the art of building sandcastles populated with caves and bridges while baking in the sun, set his original career path toward architecture rather than the law. Warren visualized creating buildings that would be an expression of the personality of a city like Pasadena which had historical vibes. A way to leave his stamp. Only after taking drawing classes did he realize his brain didn't have the artful patience to pursue that career. So instead of molding sand with his hands, Volleyball and body surfing filled his Saturday morning through Sunday night.

The day he glided on a vicious wave and got crushed by the undertow frightened and thrilled him. Smashed against the ocean's floor, unable to move for seconds, gulping for oxygen and when the undertow relaxed, he became Fearless Warren. Smiling at his friend, George, when he walked back to grab his towel.

George said, "Hey, man. You were really flying with that wave. Damn it. Wish I had your agility to ride like that."

"It's nothing. Pretty powerful stuff out there. I love it." Whacking the volleyball with his beach friends killed the remainder of the afternoon.

Later Warren rewarded himself with a strawberry frozen yogurt. Before returning home, he'd jog on the boardwalk to check out Muscle Beach. The sign identifying the space said it was originally called Santa Monica Beach Playground. In 1934, the growing local and national interest in gymnastics and strength athletes caused the name change to Muscle Beach. Warren's solid sprouting chest and arms were no match for the bulging veiny muscles modeling for the gawkers. Warren admired these bulldogs who effortlessly lifted insane-looking weights. They added a few grunts to entice the crowd. The embarrassment of enjoying the gymnastics was reduced because he was alone, and none of his friends witnessed Warren's interest.

When Warren began living at his place on Ocean Park Blvd. in 2003 while he was going to law school, his world beautifully collided with his water dreams. The location was two blocks from the beach and made driving unnecessary on the weekend. The beach alleviated the stress of studying to pass the bar. A killer exam where more than fifty percent of the applicants failed on their first time out. Warren was blessed with a photographic memory and analytical mind. Another beach perk was his daily jogging through the Venice canals shirtless, giving his chest and back acne a chance to heal. The man-made wetlands built in 1905, recreated Venice, Italy. During his jog he paid attention to the individual canal names; Altair, Cabrillo, Lion and Venus.

Having Rebecca share the small space turned it into a beach love nest. Rebecca thrived in the ocean community. Her initial reaction to Warren's furnishings brought out her diplomatic skills, "This is a great space. But now that I'm going to be living here, we need to make the most use out of each square foot. This will be my new project to freshen up the place. Make it work for us." She took Warren's hand-me-down thrift store furnishings and slowly replaced them. The dining room card table with stacking chairs got replaced by a butcher block set including matching wood with cushioned chairs. The bean bag couch got switched to a simple sleeper sofa. Paul's visits necessitated a place for him to crash for weekend escapades. Warren's relief that he liked her taste made the renovations delicious.

Warren's only-child status left him astonished at Paul and Rebecca's beautiful relationship. Besides communicating daily, never more than seven days slipped by without them connecting. Rebecca followed Paul's acting endeavors. Traveling to Long Beach, San Fernando Valley, and Ventura she watched her brother's performances in parts where he had four lines to a hefty Shakespearean supporting role in *Othello followed by* the lead in Terence McNally's play *Lisbon Traviata*.

She told Warren, "Paul is doing a revival of *Boys in The Band* at the Matrix. He invited us to opening night," or "OMG, Paul got accepted into the Groundlings Improv on Melrose. He's going to be appearing in the Sunday afternoon show."

To an outsider, their closeness that let him talk about his sexual conquests in detail would be ghoulish. Rebecca wasn't too judgmental about Paul's exploits and she welcomed the rare man whom Paul dated more than once.

"Paul, that is wonderful. I just hope you are safe. Yes, I'll check with Warren, and we'll have you guys over for dinner."

And in 2008, when the atrocious Prop Eight was on the ballot, Rebecca raised funds to fight the homophobic bill that wanted to outlaw same sex marriages. Rebecca volunteered for phone banks to drum up support for Prop Eight's defeat.

On the hellish workdays when Warren chatted up Rebecca, "I know I promised to be home for dinner, but I'm right in the middle of a declaration letter. Plus, I need to get a statement from my client for the insurance company. I may not be back until ten," her response was, "Not a problem. I'll either wait for you or have your portion ready to be heated up later."

Warren's kiss awakened Rebecca, asleep on the sofa at ten-thirty. Her smile took his breath away. While he ate turkey Bolognese and a sixteen-ingredient butter lettuce salad, she asked for details about his current case, "Sounds like you have a good chance of settlement."

"Yes, this could be big. My client fell at Brett's. Not only was there water on the floor that hadn't been wiped up but there was no sign. No warning. And get this: it was all videotaped. Of course, my client is giving me a hard time. Doesn't want to go to a chiropractor for treatment, and she hasn't been seen by a physician yet."

After dinner, Rebecca performed a deep tissue massage, the perfect closure for Saturday evening. Warren's stiff back from twelve hours of work cried for Rebecca's fingers massaging his vertebrae. Thank God tomorrow was Sunday!

The Venice Boardwalk became a Sunday morning tradition for the threesome. This was a unique weekend where Paul had bowed out at the last minute due to a late-night drinking binge the previous evening. Adult skateboarders, shirtless tattooed joggers, and animated hip hop break dancers congregated along the boardwalk. Rebecca stopped at each sunglasses vendor and kept asking Warren, "What do you think?"

"Rebecca there isn't anything that looks less than magnificent on you. Don't you have enough sunglasses?"

"I'm always losing them. Come on, let's go to Small World Books. I want to get the new Joan Didion."

Both were obsessed with reading and they easily spent an hour checking out the latest publications. Their taste ran the gamut from John Grisham to E. L. Doctorow to Alice Walker. The funky store also carried new age paraphernalia complete with incense, teas, meditation techniques, and self-help guru books. The past lives of Shirley MacLaine would have loved this space. Warren and Rebecca became suckers for the left-over hippie spirituality vibes that came with the Santa Monica Beach culture. Roots were growing to make this beach paradise permanent, but it was too small for a child, they both wanted.

During the search for Warren and Rebecca's first owned property, two elements were required. A Santa Monica zip code and anything but a boxed-in glorified apartment passing itself off as a condominium. Despite the 2008 economic downturn, Warren and Rebecca were minimally affected. Home prices and interest rates had fallen giving them an impetus to become buyers. When Joan, their agent, showed them Ocean Garden, they had to control their swooning to avoid getting a gouged price. Joan explained, "This unit usually goes for close to $800,000. It's been renovated with Bosch appliances, granite kitchen counters, laminated burnt hardwood floors, double-paned windows, and state-of-the-art bathrooms." Rebecca and Warren were gasping at the walk-in glass-enclosed shower with a jacuzzi. A patio and atrium, two car garage and two bedrooms were in perfect harmony with their family goals.

Warren thought *We've got to buy this place. It's like being in Palm Springs. No noise. It's like having our own home with the garage attached to the townhouse and separate entrances unlike a condominium. A once-in-a-lifetime purchase.*

To cinch the deal and not worry about the bank scrutinizing whether they could make the mortgage payments, Rebecca told Warren she wanted to use almost her entire inheritance from Edna on the deposit. But she still wanted to show Paul she had faith in the Reality Partnership and invested the remaining $10,000.

Warren asked, "Are you sure? The whole $290,000 on the deposit?"

"Mom would have wanted to make our life easier. I want us to enjoy ourselves. Travel and not be saddled by a huge mortgage."

The initial spurt in Warren's practice had slowed to a crawl. Getting insurance companies to pay became more challenging. Complications with insurance, worker's comp, physical therapy, and liens from doctors kept him awake at night. The pride he'd felt of always having deep REM sleeps was failing him. All contingency work so there was no payment until the case was settled in arbitration, mediation or God forbid a trial. Rebecca was spot on, acknowledging that using Edna's money would be the best way to ensure their quality of life.

Warren and Rebecca had the agent put in an offer of $725,000. The counter-offer of $735,000 guaranteed the deal. With the humongous deposit and the salaries of Warren and Rebecca, the mortgage sailed successfully to escrow closure. The landlord of their Ocean Park love nest got thirty days' notice, allowing them to skip their last month's rent. At the end of the first decade of the twenty-first century, 12-31-2009, they became owners of an Ocean Garden townhouse.

Chapter 8
The Job from Hell

Commuting via gridlocked street traffic to the Italian Home Kitchen at the Beverly Center grated on Paul. Added to that, the competition with the other waiters and waitresses about who would make it in the industry resulted in debilitating ego pain.

The weekly grind started with the calendar scheduling. Perky Veronica whispered, "Hey, I've got an audition at Paramount. Paul, can we switch nights?"

Paul wanted to ignore her. Paul's thoughts circulated around his apprenticeship at the Groundlings that had sputtered. The art of improv failed him. At last Sunday's class, the inaugural exercise was the "fortunately and unfortunately game". A back-and-forth dialogue where the players switch between fortunate and unfortunate events. Paul's on-stage partner Eugene started, "The monster was hungry for eggs"

Paul replied, "Unfortunately he forgot to peel the shells and they made him sick."

Eugene retorted "Fortunately, the monster had an iron stomach and he recovered quickly."

"Fortunately, the eggshells were salted and tasted delicious." Paul realized his mistake by not responding with an *Unfortunately*.

The other rule Paul broke during an improv game was saying "No" or asking questions to a previous statement rather than accepting and letting the scene play out.

The teacher gave them a location and goal. Carey, William and Paul were chosen. The location was a pumpkin patch and the goal was to carve a pumpkin. Carey said, "We have to carve this pumpkin before we close and I don't have a knife."

William responded, "No problem I'm going to use an ax. Paul, bring that ax to me." Paul slipped with, "No, I don't see any ax. Where did you put it, William?" Carey responded, "Paul, just grab the knife from that man sticking the knife in your back to rob you." Paul shot back, "I didn't know I was being robbed."

The teacher stopped the scene and explained what Paul was doing wrong. Paul saw the writing on the wall and quit The Groundlings. The fee of fifty dollars a month had been an impediment, too.

The crappy IHC job came to a head when he switched nights to appease Veronica. Paul's head clanged from the noise of the boisterous Thursday afternoon crowd. Philip, the busboy, called in sick forcing Paul to add clearing and cleaning the tables to his duties.

Five women celebrating the twenty-first birthday of one of their cohorts left Paul exasperated. Each guest had a dietary request, "No gluten, cheeseless pizza, leave out nuts, no chicken, only turkey, dressing on the side, and dressing mixed on the salad."

With no sleep the previous evening, Paul had zero stamina for catering to the herd of women. Paul spent last night memorizing his lines for *Dog Sees God: Confessions of a Teenage Blockhead* that would be premiering at The Hudson Theater. Because of Paul's short stature, playing a teenager in this reimagining of the Peanuts characters made for a perfect fit at age twenty-five. A midnight break found Paul hooking up with Eli from Grindr. He loved using the phone app Grindr. The app allowed members to create a personal profile and use their GPS to place them on a cascade, where they could browse other profiles sorted by distance and be viewed by nearby and faraway members depending on one's filter settings. Paul continued his life-saving question about their HIV status before his encounters even though Paul always practiced condom-safe sex. He gave his location and men available in close proximity popped up. Eli was the reward for finally nailing the lines for his acting debut at The Hudson Theater. Warren and Rebecca would be attending the opening at the end of the month and he wanted to make them proud.

Now the pounding complaints at IHC jumbled with, "I didn't order this. I thought I told you no onions. I am allergic. Can I talk to the manager? Where is my chopped salad?"

Damage control by the manager, Willie, ended with a comped entrée, and when Paul saw the credit card copy, with a zippo tip, his first thought was to run after the woman with a prodding iron asking her why there was no tip. This came a week after Paul's second offense where a party who rang up a $300 bill because of drinks and multiple orders of the highest-priced entree salmon had stiffed the restaurant. No tip for Paul, and Willie insisted that half the total be deducted from Paul's salary. Would dismissal be far off? The challenge of meeting the monthly rent of $800 had been challenging.

Rebecca's solution of investing his inheritance which would generate $2,000 a month enticed him. Paul had no head for investing. This would make his life easier. He called her after the IHC debacle telling her he was ready to commit.

Chapter 9
The Letter

Rebecca and Warren's move to Ocean Garden was completed with the precision of the components in a Swiss antique timepiece. No interruptions for utilities, internet, address changes, unpacking boxes and furniture deliveries. With Paul's help, the process that began Friday night enabled the townhouse to be up and running Monday morning. Rebecca ignored the muscle throbbing that finally eased after two days. After her major cup of Peet's coffee on Monday morning, Rebecca sat in the living room admiring her work. Never before had she been in a space that was an extension of her social buzzing Gemini personality. Without window treatments, the sun bounced directly into the living room. The reflection off the redwood floors created a sweet echo. Technicolor throw pillows on the L-shaped couch along with Kaminsky prints and the off-white walls gave the room a root vegetable earthiness. Rebecca had previously only lived in apartments. She could finally call the Ocean Garden Townhouse her first home.

Because Ocean Garden sat on the most eastern edge of Santa Monica, Warren's commute to Beverly Hills shortened and Rebecca had a two-block walk to her school.

Rebecca savored each step along Pearl Street heading to her first day of classes from her new home. Her breath soaked in the quiet neighborhood. Although only a few miles from their old Ocean Park apartment, the vibes were less beach-centric and more family oriented. The shirtless boys with surfboards were replaced with parents clutching the hands of their offspring.

Upon reaching school a familiar stinging sensation rumbled in her mouth. Her mind went to *Oh God, not another herpes outbreak.* She suspected that the stress of the move had triggered her immune system to be compromised. She had been symptom-free for two years. She wished she had a backup prescription in situations where she needed immediate relief. Doctor Resnick had suggested she take acyclovir as a prophylactic daily. If she did that an outbreak could have been prevented. Stubbornly, Rebecca had fought back not wanting to take the acyclovir as a preventative. Why put something that might be poisonous into her system unless needed? Although Doctor Resnick wanted to monitor her immune system yearly, she'd been careless in visiting her. With this new outbreak, an appointment would be warranted.

Upon arrival at school, her trip to the bathroom mirror verified she had a herpes outbreak. She called her doctor and asked for a refill to be picked up at the Rite Aid on Pico Boulevard. A short walk during her lunch break would be a quick resolution. Rebecca returned to the challenge of students looking to her to solve their communication issues.

Rebecca and Warren were blessed by the welcoming nature of the Ocean Garden's small town community. Ocean Garden had the unique ability to be self-run rather than hiring a management company. Volunteering glued the residents together. Ocean Garden turned into a co-op with weekly town halls and potluck dinners. At the same time, the spirited new decade came with riches in Warren's practice, a teaching assistant to lighten Rebecca's student load, and Paul getting within reach of being a contestant on the Emmy-winning *The Amazing Race* reality show.

He hoped it would get him career recognition after being watched by a television audience of five million. The adventure reality game show had engaged Paul and Rebecca since its debut in 2003. They had fantasized about teaming up to solve clues, navigate in exotic places like Malaysia, interact with locals, perform physical and mental challenges, and master the art of using jets, motorboats, or Uber to race to the finish line to win the million-dollar prize. Until that dream materialized, the $2,000 dividend from the American Realty Partnership investment eased the burden of killing himself working and auditioning. Rebecca repeatedly told Paul, "You don't have to keep thanking me for your monthly check. It's your money, earning interest."

June gloom had been bypassed in 2010 until the final day of the month. Fog descended on Saturday in Ocean Garden. Rebecca warned Warren about NPR reporting zero driving visibility as he kissed her and darted off. After Warren left for his once-a-month pro-bono work at the Gay and Lesbian Village, Rebecca snuggled up with her patchwork quilt, chai tea, and Jonathan Franzen's latest long-winded dysfunctional book *Freedom*. The jam-packed final weeks of school were filled with school committee meetings and two demonstrations of state-of-the-art speech enhancement therapies that had drained her. Her back took the brunt from the assault of endless sitting along with the lingering aftershock of their transplant to Ocean Garden. Her back had never completely recuperated from the establishment of the townhouse six months ago. Saturday was recovery day. She wished for a massage to extract scar tissues built up in her back. When Warren returned, she would make it a priority that he lavishes her with the same expert massage she had performed on him during law school.

When Rebecca heard the mail arrive, a single letter with an ominous unfamiliar return address from a law firm scared her.

The letter was addressed to Rebecca Burke rather than the usual Mr. and Mrs. Knight. She grabbed a letter opener and ripped open the envelope. The rattling sensation of being trapped in a vault paralyzed her as she read the contents. Her stomach felt out of balance. She wanted to destroy the foul letter but instead folded it back into the envelope and searched for a secure hiding place. The corner of the top shelf in the upstairs linen closet filled the bill. Rebecca phoned Jackie, her closest friend and compatriot at school, for advice. No answer from Jackie left Rebecca unable to concentrate on *Freedom*. Even when she tried to reheat the tea in the microwave oven, her chilly bones refused to warm.

Chapter 10
Missing Rebecca

Warren's first pro-bono assignment was Melody, a transexual at the Gay, Lesbian, Bi-sexual, Transgender (LGBT) Center. The Center was founded in 1969 in an old Victorian House on Wilshire Boulevard near downtown Los Angeles. The first non-profit in the United States with the word "gay" in its name. With growth from multi-million-dollar grants, the institution had moved to Hollywood proper, sitting on McCadden Place where Warren parked his Lexus. After Warren was escorted to a private office designated for legal counseling, he found an earthquake-trembling Melody. Melody could pass for a teenage Jennifer Aniston look-alike. The only giveaway were the large hands. Before Warren could introduce himself, Melody had started telling him the story of what happened to her, "I was in the girl's bathroom at school, sitting in a private stall. I heard laughing from the congregation of stuck-ups checking their skin and hair in the bathroom mirror. The leader of the pack, Alicia, started talking about me, 'That Melody is weird. I'll bet you anything she's a guy. That's what my younger brother told me when Melody was Melvin in sixth grade.' It got very quiet and I thought they had left. Just as I opened the door, Alicia jumped me pulling on my pants. There was a chorus of screams when they saw my genitals." Melody's breathing turned as shallow as a low tide, barely ebbing beach sand.

"Melody, do you need a break? You can tell me the rest later."

"No, I'll finish and I want this to be the last time this happens to me. Can you promise me that?"

"I'll be honest. This kind of law is new to me. If I can't handle the case then I'll get you someone else."

"So, they reported me to the principal. He told me I must use the boy's bathroom. That I was born a male and that's where I belonged. He said boys shouldn't be in the girl's room. But look at me. I would get beaten up if I went into the men's room. Now I can't use the bathroom at school."

"And what school was this?"

"It's Cold River High School in Van Nuys. It's very right-wing. I told my foster parents but they don't care."

The initial interview ended with Warren receiving enough information to move it to the next level. It had all the trappings of a Supreme Court issue. Warren's fatherly instincts turned Melody into a cub that he could protect.

Before he drove back to Ocean Garden, Warren texted Rebecca, "Anything we need before I come home?" but received no response. When he saw her red Nissan Maxima in the garage, he longed for her lavender smell upon entering the kitchen through the garage. And his fingernails and fingertips were a disaster, in need of rehabilitation by Rebecca's magic manicure.

The empty kitchen required a shout upstairs, "Rebecca I'm back from the Center." The stillness took him upstairs searching for his wife. The uncharacteristic unmade bed confounded him. No acoustics. He returned to the main floor, grabbed tortilla chips and hummus and left the townhouse. Rebecca must have been accosted by a neighbor who had diarrhea of the mouth.

The gardener Samuel, with his constant whirlpool of landscaping activities, smiled at Warren at the onset of the hunt.

"Have you seen my wife?" After shaking his head, Samuel continued his never-ending leaf blowing, pruning, and weeding of the vast Ocean Garden acreage.

Failing to find her, it occurred to Warren that Rebecca was walking her daily goal of 7,500 steps between Pearl and Ocean Park Boulevard. A whiff of anger hit Warren because she hadn't waited for his homecoming. With the lifting of the morning fog, they would have been rejuvenated together absorbing the luscious vitamin D sunlight that finally overpowered the earlier gloom. Returning to the townhouse, he sought shuteye, trying to make up for an all-nighter deadline that he'd subjected his body to earlier in the week.

When Warren woke up an hour later, he expected to see Rebecca. No messages were on his iPhone or landline voicemail. He called Paul, "Have you heard from your sister today?"

"No, in fact, I wanted to talk to her. You know that $2,000 check I receive monthly, it didn't come this week. I count on that money to make my rent which is due on the first."

"Well, when she gets back, I'll tell her. She's not answering her phone and didn't leave a note about where she was. She couldn't have gone very far because her car is still in the garage."

Paul replied, "Maybe she just needed some alone time. Anyway, I'm off to an audition at Celebration Theater. Wish me luck."

Warren tried to be positive about Paul's chances of thriving as an actor. Warren admired Paul's steely belief in achieving stardom. Warren would have relented long ago and changed professions.

Warren's edginess returned as the rolling late afternoon fog descended before sunset. Another unanswered call sent alarm bells. Warren's analytical mind looked for a clue as to her whereabouts. A call to Alexandra and Garth in number twenty-six jumped out as a solution.

"Hey, Alexandra. Did you see Rebecca today? She isn't answering her cell phone and I'm trying to figure out where she went without her car. I'm concerned."

"I did see her earlier in the afternoon. Just a quick hello. She seemed distracted. Not her usual bubbly self, but I didn't think anything of it. I'm sure she's okay. Did you hear about Ginny Lawson in number 22?"

Alexandra continued, "She died in her sleep last night. There'll be a memorial service next weekend. I know how close Rebecca was to her."

Ginny was part of the welcoming committee. She had left a red velvet chocolate cake on their front stoop with a note, *Welcome to Ocean Garden. We have a meet-and-greet on the last Sunday of the month. Please join us.* Still sprightly in her early nineties, this grand dame had jewels on each of her digits and long gray hair cascading down her back. Always wearing a red muumuu. A Hawaiian lei would have been appropriate to finish off her costume. During the meet-and-greet, she had told Rebecca and Paul, "You know, I was an opera singer in my youth. Of course, now I can hardly croak. My favorite role was Violetta in *La Traviata*." The remains of a German accent accentuated her speech patterns, giving her a world-class demeanor.

Opera wasn't a line item on their budget, but the idea of grand opera with gargantuan sets and passions flying across the stage appealed to Warren and Rebecca. When Rebecca lived with Paul, *La Traviata* looped on their CD player.

Ginny rambled on, "I have some recordings I could share with you. *"Sempre Libra"* the aria from *Traviata* always got multiple bravas.

Rebecca said, "It means *always free*."

After the meet-and-greet, Rebecca found a Maria Callas version on the free music application, Spotify. Goosebumps sprouted on their arms listening to the passionate Callas sing.

Rebecca read the English lyrics,

Always free and aimless I frolic
From joy to joy
Flowing along the surface
Of life's passage

Ginny became an honorary mom to Warren and Rebecca. Her opera stories were filled with juicy details. An overweight Birgit Nilsson doing *Tosca* was the most memorable. In the final scene, she leaped out a window, plunging to her death. The director had the set designer build a window facing the back of the stage. Birgit with her back to the audience jumped through the window and landed on a mattress to give the illusion of really diving to her death. Unfortunately, when the soprano landed on the mattress she bounced up in full view of the audience.

Both Rebecca and Warren made house calls before shopping at the local Trader Joe's if Ginny needed any sustenance. Rebecca brought her luscious leftovers. Rebecca and Ginny had meshed into a spiritual bond, filling the gap since Edna died.

During their weekly late afternoon licorice tea and clotted cream scone refreshment Rebecca said, "What's your secret to staying so youthful? I hope I'll look like you when I get to be ninety. And you still have all your faculties. I'm worried that I'll inherit the dementia that was part of the reason why my mom died so young."

"Yes, I bit the bullet about not catching Alzheimer's. I guess I got my suffering out of the way when I was young. Now I am reaping the benefits."

"What do you mean, Ginny?"

"I'd fallen in love with a Jewish boy named Karl in 1940. I had just turned twenty. His family had been taken to Auschwitz, yet he had escaped. He never explained how that happened. I suspect because he had blonde hair and blue eyes, no one questioned him. He could pass as a pure-bred German."

"How did you meet?"

"At University I saw him smoking in the courtyard. I was rushing to class and when he caught my eye, I stared at him, lost my balance, tripped and fell. He quickly came to my rescue. I couldn't stop looking at his gold-plated hair and trusting blue eyes. The intensity and desperation chilled me. I had my first crush. We met after school every day, held hands, kissed and talked about literature. Tolstoy's *Crime and Punishment* gave us hours of discussion. For music, Wagner dominated our lives. We fought about his best work. Was it *The Ring* or *The Flying Dutchman or Tristan and Isolde*? We had no idea he was anti-Semitic. This went on for five glorious months."

"Sounds like a fairy tale."

"I wish. He told me he had been living with an uncle who had just been taken to a concentration camp and now he needed a place to stay. So, I begged my parents to let him stay in our house."

"Did you tell your parents he was Jewish?"

"Not at first. They wanted to know where his family was. They were suspicious when I didn't answer them. Plus, my father didn't think it was appropriate for a boy to be staying at our house. And when I kept hounding them about letting him stay, I think it made it worse. They could see I was in love."

Ginny's eyes drizzled. Rebecca said, "How horrible. I remember that feeling of first love. The way I felt about Warren and it confused me."

"I told them Karl's parents were murdered in Auschwitz. I begged my parents to let him hide in our house even though I knew how dangerous it would be. And when Papa refused, I shut myself in my room. My parents kept pleading with me to understand why he couldn't live with us. When I met up with Karl to tell him, he was devastated. He wanted me to run away with him."

"Oh God, what did you do?"

"I told him yes. He said to meet him at the Central Berlin Train Station at midnight. That evening I started packing my clothes and snuck out of the house to rendezvous with Brett. I had no idea what his plans were or where we would be going. I was so in love. I'd never felt this way before."

"You must have been so scared."

"When I got to the station it was deserted. I wasn't even sure trains would be running that late. I waited and waited and waited. Brett never showed up. I was worried about being out alone in the early morning hours. I went back home and tried to sleep. I planned to look for Brett at school the next day."

"Did he explain why he didn't show up?"

"I never heard from him again. He had vanished."

Ginny stopped abruptly then continued, "My life changed after that. I became obsessed with music and singing. I never gave myself time to mourn my relationship with Karl. I married later when I moved to America but it wasn't the same kind of love and we divorced after ten years. We never had children. My career came first. Enough about me. I don't want to wallow in the past."

Rebecca's brimming tears commiserated with Ginny and cemented their friendship. Rebecca understood Ginny's denial of mourning. Rebecca hadn't come to terms with her own mother's death.

After Alexandra's news about Ginny's death, Warren's windpipe began tightening, realizing the impact it would have on Rebecca. He whimpered, "Goodbye, Alexandra" and rushed to the kitchen for water to unclog his throat. The exhaustion of looking for Rebecca lulled him into another short siesta on the sofa.

Roaming through the townhouse, aimlessly checking for Rebecca again, Warren imagined that upon waking, Rebecca had returned. A noise emanating from upstairs made Warren climb the staircase. Operatic tones got louder when he entered their bedroom. The angle of the bunched-up comforter made Warren cry, "Rebecca, are you hiding from me?" He couldn't determine the source of the music. How odd that it was the familiar Verdi aria from *La Traviata*. The melody swam in his head, building to a crescendo. He checked the walk-in closet and felt a figure trying to escape. A moth searching for a flame. Was it Ginny or Rebecca tricking him?

Warren headed towards the rarely used small balcony attached to the master bedroom. Earlier in the year, a robin had made a nest in the top corner of the balcony where they witnessed the building of a nest and caring for the baby robins. The welcoming morning chirping became a natural alarm clock to awaken them. Smiling when thinking about the day they would have their own young to care for. The crushing blow when the chirping stopped made them realize the young robins could fly on their own. The nest would be abandoned until the mating season arrived in a year.

From the balcony jutting out of their neighbor's place across from their townhouse came the mellifluous sounds of *La Traviata*. Violetta's cry of freedom honored Ginny's memory. Warren breathed in the tones from the CD. He thought about Ginny and the love she showered on them. He had to find Rebecca.

Chapter 11
The Rescue

Rebecca sat with her freshly squeezed lemonade at Urth Café on Main Street, rejuvenated by the tangy sweet and sour liquid. The twinge in her leg muscles signaled that she needed a breather. A wistful break before the sun folded into the ocean. Rebecca remembered she had promised Ginny carrot cake from Urth Café. Her mouth whipped into a frenzy looking at the pineapple and golden raisins in the dessert. The murkiness about her last Ginny visit seized Rebecca when she paid for the dessert. A premonition about Ginny reflecting her age frightened Rebecca.

The two-hour walk along Ocean Park Boulevard had left her energy shattered. Rebecca pretended to be a runaway child, escaping responsibility. In fact, when she passed their previous address on Ocean Park Boulevard, she longed to knock on the door and see what the new tenants had done to their love nest. She wanted to take a time machine back to their old life where the shouting distance to the ocean would revive her daily. The two-mile gap from her current address at Ocean Garden ached her. She'd missed the joggers and bikers on the beachside path since the move. The bustle of Main Street with vegetarian eateries and hippie boutiques contrasted with their sedate Pearl Street location. For foodie Rebecca, Dhaba Cuisine of India topped her must-eat restaurant list. She used to wander through The California Heritage

Museum housed in a Victorian home after grabbing gourmet delicacies from food trucks or the weekly Farmer's Market. She vowed to return to this fantasy world regularly.

Reality pounced back. She rehearsed what she would tell Warren and prayed that he would liberate her from the pang of remorse that was brewing.

You know the venture that I had Paul invest his money in? The inheritance from Mom. I received a letter from the partnership. It's gone bankrupt. Actually, it was a Ponzi scheme. And since the 2008 financial collapse, property values have plunged. Lawyers are handling the dissolution but according to the letter, there won't be much money left to give back to the investors.

Paul is going to kill me. He invested his entire inheritance of $300,000. I feel like shit. He was counting on the interest to live on. Thank goodness we only put $10,000 in. The rest we used for the down payment on the townhouse. But we can afford to lose that kind of money. Paul can't. I'm his older sister and I'm supposed to be taking care of him. How am I going to tell him, Warren?

She'd be a disappointment to both Paul and Warren. Warren had warned her and she ignored him. She wanted Paul to have the financial means to allow him to focus on his acting career.

The descending darkness and early evening chill meant she needed Warren to rescue her. The iPhone came to life, clogged with texts and messages from Warren and Paul. She let her diaphragm push her breath, giving her the energy to call Warren. She texted her location to Warren.

A short blink and a mirage of Warren's Lexus appeared. Her slayer of dragons left the car and ran into Rebecca's defeated arms. An embrace that refused to end. No words. He let her cry. This fetching man had brought healing powers to Rebecca.

After Rebecca recuperated, Warren explained, "Don't worry about Paul. We'll tell him together. And look, we have that second bedroom if he needs to move in with us. If he doesn't have to pay for rent, he'll be fine."

"You're sure, Warren. Paul can be a handful."

"No, it's fine. And it will be good for you when I work late. You'll have his company." Warren held in the news about Ginny until he felt Rebecca could handle her death.

When they returned to the townhouse, Rebecca told Warren, "I brought Ginny's favorite dessert. I'm going to run over to her place while it's fresh. Did you want to come?"

Warren's eyes wrenched her gut when he spoke. The flooding memories of her mom congealed with Ginny's death ripped off Rebecca's mourning guard rails. Warren, her savior, had to work overtime to patch Rebecca together.

Chapter 12
Warren, Paul and Rebecca

Within a couple of months, Paul checked out of his Silverlake apartment. Ten years of his life passed during the packing of his meager possessions. Rooming with Rebecca had come full circle. It had been five years since Rebecca had been his roommate and now he would be occupying the second bedroom in Paul and Rebecca's Ocean Garden townhome. She knew how to prop him up. She had become a rehearsing partner for auditions. He referred to Rebecca as his stage manager. When he couldn't get to the guts of a character, Rebecca was a sounding board. The play *Broken* which took place during the AIDS crisis challenged Warren. The drama dealt with infidelity. Playing the character of Gary who believed in monogamy left Warren clueless.

Paul couldn't imagine having a single partner. He'd feel incarcerated if deprived of a variety of men. With Rebecca's prodding, he carved a hole into the essence of the character of "Gary" and won the part at The Met Theater.

After Rebecca married in 2005, the cavalcade of lodgers willing to share the rent gave Paul a chance to meet and fuck a diverse group of guys. He was gung-ho with his choices of chubby, stick thin, way taller than his five foot eight or as small as five foot three men. And the cultural range of Asian, Latino, Black and Middle Eastern expanded his worldview along with culinary expertise all over the globe. He learned the art of making dim sum, sweet potato pie, mouth-watering falafels and the green corn tamales that were better than the classic version at the restaurant, El Chollo. So, he needed to be patient to let the culture shock of Santa Monica regenerate him.

His comfort level with Santa Monica had grown. He no longer felt like an alien because of the lack of gay sensibility. Also, a shortage of bars would cut down on his hookups. No equivalent to his favorite eatery, Casita Del Campo on Hyperion. He hoped the elimination of sexual distractions was a good omen. The distance from Hollywood auditions needed to be overcome. Congested traveling east on the Santa Monica Freeway required careful planning to make appointments. The almost non-existent theater scene was barely saved by The Odyssey, Santa Monica Playhouse, and Morgan-Wixson Community Theater on the west side. Still, there was the joy of living with his sister and brother-in-law. Never feeling like a third wheel. Even the improved air quality made him hopeful about his acting profession.

Convincing Rebecca that she wasn't responsible for his nest egg destruction took repeated conversations, "It's not your fault. You didn't know we would be going into a great recession. You should blame your friend at school for telling you about it."

Paul took on the responsibility of housekeeping including cooking their meals. A fair exchange for free rent. And between the pool and tennis court on the grounds, he had a damn good setup. Well almost. The blow torch to the arrangement came down to sexual activity after a year of living with Warren and Rebecca. Paul knew his free ride couldn't last indefinitely.

Early on there had been an arrangement. First Rebecca privately told Paul, "You know we love having you here, but there are times we're going to need some privacy. I think you know where I am going."

"I get it. You want me to spend the night with some stranger? Something you are trying to stop me from doing?"

She laughed and pushed him away. Paul enjoyed Rebecca's honesty and felt emboldened by her suggestion that allowed him free reign until the incident with Warren.

It was initiated when Paul visited Rage in West Hollywood. The twenty-something crowd called "twinkies" were out in force. Paul ducked into Rage, grabbed a Corona, and danced to Katy Perry's 'California Girls." The deaf-inducing audible level didn't stop him from chatting with a sweet catch matching Paul's five foot eight. The boy's jeans and tee-shirt were squashing his package giving new meaning to skintight. Paul swooned after discovering his name was Joshua. Mona Lisa would be jealous of Joshua's eyes that never stopped worshiping Paul. The midnight chime elicited Paul's conversation, "I've had enough. Can we go back to your place?"

He said, "Sorry, No. I'm still living with my parents. After I graduated from West Side University, between the student loans and lack of decent paying jobs, using my political science degree forced me to live with Mom and Dad. Since the recession, government jobs have dried up. What about your place?"

"I don't know. I'm living with my sister and her husband in Santa Monica."

"Oh, come on. We could go to the beach Sunday morning. Very cool."

"Well, if you behave yourself, I guess it could work."

Joshua took his car and followed Paul to Ocean Garden. The easy drive with Rhianna's 'Only Girl in the World" packing a wallop in Paul's Mustang, set the stage for Paul's latest conquest. This was the first time he'd brought a trick to his new home. He assumed Rebecca and Warren would be okay with the practice since they hadn't expressly forbidden him from bringing guests to Ocean Garden.

Quietly entering the townhouse and creeping up the stairs like thieves, made the plopping onto Paul's double bed without incident a milestone. Paul had to continually shush Joshua while they began snacking foreplay that evolved into a main entrée of lovemaking.

Their elongated sleep ended with the fragrance of breakfast floating up to the second floor. The sizzling bacon and French toast hit their nostrils.

After the knock on the bedroom door came Rebecca's voice, "Hey Paul. It's almost ten. Did you want to join us for breakfast?"

"Sure, we'll be right down. Give us about ten minutes."

Paul hoped that using the pronoun "we" clued Rebecca that he had a guest. After a quick shower without time to shave, they headed downstairs.

Warren's face tried to hold back the shock of meeting Joshua.

The introductions were civil. Rebecca was used to the drill when they were roommates, never knowing what surprise visitor would accompany Paul home. But now as a married woman with Warren by her side, the rules of engagement had changed. The bristling undertone annoyed Paul.

Warren was speechless until Rebecca looked at Joshua and said, "Would you like some coffee?"

Warren remained mute when Joshua innocently responded with, "Oh, God, that would be great. You have a lovely home."

Paul interrupted, "You know I think we're going out for breakfast. I wanted to show Joshua the Abbot Kinney area." Abbot Kinney was a stylish street, home to magnificent boutiques, galleries, coffee shops (Butcher's Daughter) and restaurants (The

Tasting Kitchen). The Westside's hippest haven, offering twenty-four hours of beach-adjacent exploration.

Paul and Joshua disappeared in a flash.

Paul should not have been surprised when Warren told him the following day, "Rebecca won't tell you, but you can't bring guys here. And Rebecca told me your history of picking up men. I feel uncomfortable with a stranger staying here."

Paul had been off to the Diamond Fitness Gym and Warren barricaded the door. He found the alone time with Warren similar to petting a ferocious lion; fearful that his closeted attraction to Warren would result in a catastrophe. He didn't want this encounter to be the tipping point.

Paul replied, "Look, I can tell if someone is dangerous. I've never had a problem before."

Warren's astonishment at Paul's innocence left him angry.

"I don't care about your gut feeling. It's unacceptable. You're under our roof. You aren't paying rent so you need to follow our rules."

"I do my share here. I clean up after your mess and cook your meals. Maybe it's time for me to move out so I can have some privacy."

When Paul tried to exit, Warren gently used his arms to stop him, "I know. We appreciate what you do and you're good for Rebecca. I'm such a workaholic. The law is like a mistress."

"You know Warren, you may think Rebecca is this really strong woman, but you are missing a hidden fragility. Don't you worry that it's an act? You really should spend more time with her. I thought with me helping with chores, you'd have that time."

Warren reached out to Paul and hugged him. The embrace simmered through both of them almost to the point of being transformative. Paul hadn't realized the need to be accepted by his brother-in-law.

Chapter 13

The Baby Maker

Initially, Dr. Resnick had unkind words at Rebecca's appointment on January 2, 2012.

"I'm disappointed that you haven't come in for at least an annual physical. You know we are watching your immune system. I don't want to worry you. And things have been okay up until now, but it's important." Thankfully, an underlying warmth emanating from Dr. Resnick brought Rebecca solace.

"Is something wrong with my blood work?"

"Not really. A few of your numbers are out of range, blood cell related. We are also looking at chemicals that are red flags—these have been concerning. And this herpes outbreak could impact your numbers."

"I know you wanted me to take acyclovir daily as a preventive."

"No, that's fine. This time make a follow-up appointment for six months."

"Is there anything I can take for my back? I must have pulled back muscles when we got settled in our new home, but it's still bothering me. Anti-inflammatory pills haven't worked."

"Let's be conservative and try physical therapy before we do any invasive radiology work."

"Thanks. Oh, before I go, we were thinking about having children. I don't have anything to worry about, do I?"

"Sure, go ahead. And it's good that you're young, less risky. You're thirty, right? That's when I had my first child. How long have you been married?"

"Almost seven years. Why do you ask?"

"There was an old superstition about the seven-year itch. Really, I always want the decision to have children to be joint and after the marriage has cemented. Too many couples jump the gun about children and regret the outcome."

Rebecca had no qualms about children and even though Warren didn't jabber about it, she was convinced he had fatherhood in his blood.

Upon returning to Ocean Garden at five, Rebecca found Warren in the kitchen preparing dinner. Rebecca was giddy at the prospect of Warren being home from work early.

"Is everything okay? I'm shocked to see you home at a normal hour. And where is Paul? I thought he was making Cornish game hens tonight."

"He had an audition, and I wanted to cook for you."

Rebecca said, "I've got a present for you. Let's go upstairs."

Warren ran after Rebecca as she hastily ascended the steps, screaming, "I'm gonna get you."

Warren and Rebecca stripped and fell into bed. Warren tickled her feet until Rebecca purred, "I got the okay from my doctor. Are you ready to make a baby?"

"Damn you, woman. I've been so ready. You're going to be the mother of the year."

"Okay, this is a practice run. Tomorrow, I stop taking the pill." While Warren ravished Rebecca, he didn't let his fears about fatherhood corrupt the afternoon delight.

Getting pregnant wasn't all that easy. They tried different positions. Sex in the morning rather than the evening. Right after her period stopped or a week later. Warren suggested having sex multiple times on the same day, thinking there would be so much sperm in Rebecca it would surely find an egg to fertilize. The baby-making process was malfunctioning. Rebecca tried diets that included more antioxidants, less refined carbs, more fiber and high-fat dairy. Each of their doctors said they were healthy. Warren's sperm count was excellent and Rebecca passed her fertility blood tests.

Warren and Rebecca agreed about no In vitro fertilization, donated sperm, eggs or embryos. Rebecca told the doctor, "No." when Intrauterine Insemination was proposed where sperm cells were inserted directly into the womb during ovulation.

After a year of trying, they talked about adopting. Rebecca's doctor said, "Give yourself a rest; stop trying so hard, and you'll be surprised at the result." A long vacation was the prescription with three weeks in Vietnam during the Christmas break. The Southeast paradise was the consensus of their friends who had visited Vietnam.

After they recovered from the severe jet lag of 14 hours of flying, they decided to explore the city of Saigon which had been renamed Ho Chi Minh City. The cars swirled in the streets without braking. The motorcycle women had long white gloves and masks. The autos and bikes were oblivious to pedestrians.

"Warren, how am I going to cross?"

"Just look like you know where you are going. They'll get out of the way."

She slowly marched into the speeding avenue with eyes barely open. She pretended she was blind and darted into the road.

"Go, Rebecca. Move. Just walk, walk!!" Warren hollered.

Her heart wanted to burst. Her frightened feet said, *Forget it. You are going to be run over.* Gobbled nerves swallowed blasting horns. *Oh God, that car was swerving towards me.* She jumped.

"Come on."

She saw her cheerleader Warren shouting, "Yes, yes, you're almost there." She fell into his body.

"This is so third world. Why did I ever agree to coming here?"

"It's an adventure, honey."

The vacation began in Ho Chi Minh City and they worked their way north to Hanoi. The luxury of a private tour compensated for Vietnam's third-world status. The healthy and delicious diet of jackfruit, broken rice and tableside barbecue fish satisfied their gourmet desires. Inimitable eating at cooking schools surprised Warren and Rebecca. Removing the baby maker sexual component converted them into playful cuddly like doggies in heat. But behind the scenes, Rebecca was using a visualization technique she had learned in college. If she could visualize Warren getting her pregnant, it would become a reality. Rebecca believed this was the last holiday she would take for years, once she became a mother. The words of Dr. Resnick had been haunting her, like an itch that no matter how much you scratched, the itch never went away. Rebecca, who usually never catastrophized, thought Vietnam would be the last trip she would ever take. And if that were true, each moment had to be tattooed into her brain, so she could not forget sights and smells.

After becoming experts at conquering traffic in Ho Chi Minh City, Hanoi was effortless. Nearby Ha Long Bay was a two-day break from the bustling Hanoi. The emerald waters, limestone islands, and rainforests were the pinnacle of their vacation. They spent the night in a junk boat with two other couples. Rebecca and

Warren learned that junk boats were a type of Chinese sailing ship with fully battened sails that looked like large accordion fans.

The romanticism of the embroidered teak, oak walls and furniture was easy to savor. Dining on the deck while watching the sunset threw Rebecca and Warren into a vision of heaven.

The next evening, they took an overnight train to Sapa, the most northern edge of Vietnam bordering China.

Eight hours later they arrived in Sapa. The first image of Sapa entailed an unaccompanied large boar trampling down the street. The chilly air mixed with a stupendous mountain view filled up their corneas and nostrils.

They spent the next two days hiking where they viewed tiered rice paddies that created a wiggly design into the sweeping mountain valleys filled with hilltop villages.

On the third night, they repeated the train excursion back to Hanoi.

The train puffed into Hanoi at five in the morning. Warren scouted the town for an authentic pho breakfast that would include rice noodles with chicken, ginger, cinnamon, onion, and star anise. Rebecca and Warren posed as Vietnamese sitting with the crowd inhaling the steeping hot brilliant broth. Outside the restaurant window, a mysterious line of sweet marauders stood by Hanoi Lake.

The sun hadn't risen and moonlight was the only illumination. Warren and Rebecca came to realize groups of Vietnamese were performing Tai Chi. It was like watching symphony players that moved to the rhythmic exercise.

During their final night in Hanoi before flying back to Santa Monica, Rebecca said, "You know my period is two weeks late. I'm pretty regular."

Warren grinned, "That's good news. Maybe all we needed to procreate was Vietnam."

"Don't talk like that. I don't want to jinx it. I've been nauseous too. Hope I didn't pick anything up when we ate from the street food last night."

"But the mixture of fish marinating in lime juice, herbs and chili were delicious."

"You have an iron stomach, Warren. Anyway, I've been to the bathroom way too much."

"Just think of it as a foreshadowing of morning sickness."

Within a week of their homecoming to civilization, Rebecca's pregnancy test returned positive results. Warren and Rebecca had a roaring celebration to coincide with the new year. 2014.

Chapter 14
Paul and Joshua

Since Paul's sexual exploits were barricaded from Ocean Garden, his selection of conquests became limited. The embarrassing interrogation began with, "Do you have your own place?" Paul's financial restrictions made sharing an apartment unattainable. *The Amazing Race* gig had never materialized. A pity party wasn't too far off until his Uncle Buddy made his weekly call checking up on Paul, and a plan was hatched. The halfway meeting point between Silverlake and Santa Monica was at Third and Fairfax Farmers Market in The Grove.

Paul's rule of following the Sondheim song, "I Never Do Anything Twice" had been broken with Joshua. The political science addict moved to the top of Paul's dance card when Joshua left his parent's nest and shared a mini-two bedroom with another political junkie, Freddy, in West Hollywood.

Even with Paul's rollercoaster dating pattern, Joshua asked Paul in West Hollywood's Italian eatery, Marco's, "What would you think about moving into my apartment?" The trattoria had gut-busting Lobster Macaroni and Cheese with sauteed mushrooms and truffles. The smell of the dish reverberated when it landed on the table. Paul stretched each of his fingers repeatedly to distract from Joshua's eyelashes that tried to manipulate him.

Famished Paul said, "Let's eat first, and then we can talk about this."

"I thought you'd be excited. I know you've been wanting to move away from your sister and controlling brother-in-law."

Paul ignored his growling abdomen. "It's so small. And we'd have no privacy with your roommate, Fred."

"You're wrong. Fred has an out-of-town assignment writing a column for The San Francisco Chronicle. They had been following Fred's work when he was at Berkley and thought it was perfect to get a perspective on the differences between Los Angeles and San Francisco."

"So, he's moving out?"

"No, he wants to keep the place in case the job doesn't work out. Plus, he's so used to living here; he couldn't imagine staying in San Francisco."

Joshua's exuberance tempted Paul to agree to the plan. At least Joshua had retired any thoughts of heavy-duty romance. But after a recent sexual session with Joshua, a frightening vulnerability kicked in triggered by Joshua's resurfacing of, *"I love you."* It provoked a hidden scream.

When Paul's interior yelp subsided, he said "Joshua, you are young. You don't want to fall in love with me. I'm not willing to be monogamous, and I know you want that."

Joshua shot back, "Okay, I'll just use Tina Turner's song 'What's Love Got to Do with It" as my mantra."

Paul set up a lunch with his Uncle Buddy where he would update him about Joshua's proposal; Paul hoped Buddy would give him guidance to solve the conundrum. When he saw Buddy's wrinkle-free face and sprightly walk, Paul said, "Are you like Dorian Gray with a portrait hidden in your closet that looks your age?"

Buddy laughed, "Yes, Oscar Wilde used my prototype for his novel."

"Tell me the magic trick, Uncle."

"Don't follow the boring rules about doing everything in moderation. It's bullshit. Just enjoy yourself. Don't take things seriously and brush your teeth. Your teeth are the major component of smiling which is the window to your soul. And finally, never ever stop having sex even if you have to use Viagra."

The maître 'd asked where they wanted to sit, "Is there room on the patio?" The patio faced a grove of trees. Paul never tired of Italian delicacies. He craved the homemade spaghetti, spumoni and bruschetta and ordered immediately after they were seated.

Buddy jumped the gun, "So what is going on? You sounded on the verge of a mini-breakdown when we spoke, and you set this up."

"Oh, I was just having one of my drama queen episodes."

"Boy trouble, acting, my niece Rebecca, Warren?"

Paul responded, "It's about Joshua. How is it that you've lived all these years without having a boyfriend? Unless you had somebody before I was born."

Buddy laughed, "It's leftovers from an ancient era that I grew up in where homosexuality was outlawed. You could say I'm the perennial bachelor. Sounds like a Rock Hudson or Cary Grant, hiding behind that terminology. At least I never resorted to having a beard."

"What's that?"

"Oh, a trophy girlfriend or, in Hollywood, a wife for show. To go to premieres or parties. Thank God, those times are over and we have Ian Mc Kellan and Matt Bomer. Out actors unafraid of losing popularity or roles because they are gay. But back to you, what is the issue with Joshua?"

"He wants me to move in with him. You know I thought once we'd gotten over the *I love you* stuff that cohabiting would be off the table." Buddy knew about Paul's resistance to declaring those three words.

"Well, it would be a good opportunity to separate from Rebecca and Paul. Are they still hassling you about tricks spending the night?"

"I've been trying to be a good boy, so it hasn't come up again."

"Oh, I think I understand. You wanted to move into my Victorian palace."

"Would that be so awful? We get along and we're both sluts."

The food arrived and gave Paul a chance to admire the waiter. Clyde had a scar gouged into his cheek giving him the stamp of a dangerous boxer. His arm muscles were begging to be free from his tight starched white uniform. Clyde delved into Paul with, "This is my favorite dish. Enjoy. Let me know if there is anything else you want." When Clyde touched Paul's shoulder, he could swear Clyde had X-rayed him.

Buddy laughed, "You are incorrigible. I've heard of making love with your eyes but it looked like he was ready to consensually rape you."

"So, will you think about me as a roommate?"

"I would have, but I've decided to get out of Los Angeles and move to Palm Springs. They have a well-connected gay community along with an art museum and legitimate theater. Just bad timing."

Paul replied, "Well now I'll have a place to visit in Palm Springs," without showing any disappointment.

During the meal finale, Paul had secured Clyde's phone number. The timing of Paul's ringing iPhone when they departed the restaurant elicited Buddy's observation, "That was quick."

Paul shushed Buddy as Rebecca spoke, "You're going to be an uncle, Paul."

"Wow. Congratulations, sister. That's great news. I know you've been trying for a long time."

So, God had decided that in less than nine months Paul would be evicted and forced to live with Joshua. He imagined Rebecca making plans to fumigate the second bedroom and ready it for a little Knight. Paul searched for an upside to sharing an apartment with Joshua. Living in Joshua's Westbourne apartment, the WeHo address would be returning to his roots that Dorothy in *Wizard of Oz* encountered when she returned to Kansas. WeHo would always be home rather than Santa Monica Oz.

A rush of emotion surprised Paul. He nosedived into tears driving away. He had been missing his mom, and with Buddy moving to Palm Springs and a physical separation from Rebecca and Warren, he worried about feeling abandoned.

Chapter 15
Uncle Buddy

Buddy slowly drove home. He didn't want to tell Paul the actual reason for the move. It would get back to Rebecca and now that she was pregnant, he did not want her to be alarmed.

Two months ago, while driving back from a non-alcoholic afternoon birthday party at Casita Del Campo, he heard a loud thump after turning the corner at Effie and Hyperion. What had he hit? Was it a cat or dog darting into the road? He pulled his Accord towards the curb, parked and looked behind the car. He had trouble focusing until he saw a crumbled man lying in the street which caused Buddy to quiver. How did he not see this man? What was wrong with him? Buddy rushed towards the body, craving for movement. He bent down ready to breathe life into the still torso.

"Are you all right? I am so sorry. I didn't see you."

The unscathed man with honey blonde highlights scraped himself from the pavement. The dazed and confused look killed Buddy. His brain filled up with thoughts of being accused of attempted manslaughter.

"Should we call an ambulance? Do you want me to drive you to the emergency room?"

"Didn't you see me crossing the street? I wasn't jaywalking."

Buddy noticed that the man's cell phone lay splattered on the ground, snatched it for him and said, "I'll replace your iPhone if it doesn't work."

"I can't believe you didn't see me."

"I'm sorry. I wasn't texting or using my phone. Are you going to be okay?"

"I'm just a little shaken up. I didn't break anything. I don't even think I'm bruised."

Buddy kept repeating to himself *Thank God* until his pulse stopped agitating.

"Let me know if there is anything I can do. Replace your cell phone. You may have a delayed reaction and be sore."

"I'll be fine. Just pay attention when you are driving. Give me your phone and I'll enter my email address and phone number so you can reach me."- Jonathan Erickson @ yahoo.com 323-688-2986.

Buddy crawled back to his Accord, unsettled but temporarily relieved. Back at his apartment, mortified Buddy needed consoling, but he was humiliated to call friends or family. Buddy's eighty years had caught up with him. In the past year a series of dings to his car should have been a warning. Buddy had become a sloppy driver, hitting poles or grating his Accord against the walls in parking structures. The fear of giving up his driver's license would begin a descent to worthlessness.

Buddy's ballooning checklist of nightmare scenarios started with *Jonathan has internal bleeding and has to be hospitalized* then moved to *Jonathan dies or is permanently disabled* and *finally, police knocking at the door and they're going to arrest me.*

Binging *House of Cards* distracted him through the remainder of the polluted afternoon. Buddy had avoided a visit to his primary care physician other than annual physicals, but now that was no longer an option.

The squeezed-in quick appointment with Dr. Feldstein brought solace because the doctor became Buddy's confessor. Feldstein had been his gay-friendly doctor for forty years. Buddy was able to talk about his sexuality, prostate, impotency, hormones, and gay male medical concerns. Because Feldstein was so knowledgeable and in tune, Buddy suspected he was part of the same tribe from his first visit. So, when he saw him in his Saturday morning poetry class at the Gay and Lesbian Village in Hollywood, the surprise factor was subdued. Feldstein said, "We know each other, don't we?" Buddy acknowledged with a smile. In future appointments, the awkwardness of their doctor-patient relationship was endearing.

He told Feldstein, "I am very concerned because I've become very accident-prone. I accidentally hit a pedestrian on Sunday. I was worried I'd seriously injured him, but I lucked out. He was unhurt. At home, I keep banging into cabinets, too."

"Are you distracted, having a hard time concentrating?"

"No, I thought I was paying attention. It was as though the man was invisible. I hadn't realized I'd hit someone until I heard a horrible noise."

"Besides these accidents you've had with your car and the cabinets, has anything else been going on?"

"No, I've been a little more forgetful, but I'm eighty. I have to be careful when I'm walking. My legs have been feeling rubbery."

"Okay, I'm going to send you to a neurologist. They can do some testing and see if anything is wrong. Nothing to worry about. As you said, it's part of the fun of aging. It might be depression that could be affecting you."

Two days later Buddy made a follow-up call to Jonathan, "I wanted to see how you are doing."

"Thank you for calling. It means a lot to me. And yes, I'm fine."

"What about your iPhone?"

"Don't worry about that. I'm just glad I wasn't hurt."

Buddy hoped he'd been given a second chance. He would make an extreme effort to slow down and pay attention to details.

Sadly, within a month he was diagnosed with mild cognitive impairment. The MRI revealed brain atrophy and after extensive sixteen-hour memory testing, the possibility of dementia became a reality. The neurologist cursed him with, "We need to watch those symptoms you mentioned about your legs feeling rubbery. That could be a sign of Louie Body dementia which affects motor function." The curse his sister Edna died from was galloping into Buddy's life.

He didn't want Paul and Rebecca to witness his decline and that made the move to Palm Springs the perfect solution. Buddy had researched Memory Care units, which were affordable in Palm Springs, in the event he eventually needed that care. The lower cost of living made Palm Springs enticing. The neurologist explained, "This is a degenerative disease. There is no cure and I can't promise you any of the drugs available can slow the progression. And I should warn you that the speed of cognitive decline is unknown." Buddy was resigned to the future tobogganing journey on his own terms.

The conversation with his nephew triggered Buddy's regret that he didn't have a husband or lover, or intimate best friend. Buddy's motto of being his own best friend had bitten him in the ass. Buddy had remorse that he had given Paul a guidebook that excluded the words *I Love You*. That consolation prize would elude both of them. With the closely knit desert gay community, Buddy would dare himself to fall in like, with another man. He wanted to stretch out his remaining years when he was fully cognitive.

Chapter 16
Teaching

The stress of teaching and being pregnant was taking its toll on Rebecca. The barrage of students that she handled was a dam ready to burst. Each year new teaching techniques were mandated. She was burdened by computer programs to learn and the legality of threatened malpractice that pounded speech therapists daily. Parents were the monsters in the room.

She was formally addressed by parents:

"Mrs. Knight, did you tell Erica that she shouldn't use slang? Cultural references shouldn't be condemned. I want her to be proud of her heritage. And if that means using what you call slang, I will not have that suppressed."

"Mrs. Knight, did you touch Johnny during your session? You know it's inappropriate to touch a child. He said you were feeling his throat. Something about how his vocal cords work. And when you were explaining speech patterns your hands were circling his mouth. I don't know why you need to do that. I should report you to the authorities. Please stop doing that."

Rebecca's hormones had been out of whack three months into her pregnancy. Rebecca began to worry about her immune system because her students were sent to school ill and the germs could give her pneumonia. And then the parents called, "Mrs. Knight we hired a private speech therapist and they disagreed with your approach. The goals at your school don't match the guidelines for Angie."

The final cesspool event came when Rebecca was with her teacher cohorts in their monthly meeting. The head of the department told the group, "I'd like to introduce you to Mr. Benjamin Holst. He's an attorney from Lewis, Epstein and Klein and he'll be rewriting your speech reports. This is a new practice so we don't get sued by parents."

Rebecca exploded, "But they know nothing about speech. How can you do this?" Rebecca's closeted temper got unleashed. She stood up and left the meeting, leaving the room stunned in silence. Even her good friend Jackie was flabbergasted at Rebecca's action.

When Warren found her at the empty dining room table that evening blankly staring, he thought she was an apparition. The pregnancy glow had faded.

"Rebecca. You don't look like yourself. What happened?"

"Oh, Warren. I've had enough with the teaching. It's too difficult. The pressure and now they have attorneys checking our work. I'm tired of fighting the system. It's been over ten years. Enough to get vested for my pension. I'm worried about the baby."

Rebecca was afraid to admit that not only had the added weight caused her already fragile back to flare up, but her energy level was at zero. She hoped leaving her job would revive her.

Warren took Rebecca's hands, "Don't worry. You need to take care of yourself. Plus, I'm making enough money that you don't need to work."

"But I used to love what I was doing. I'm disappointed in myself."

"Come on, babe. Don't beat yourself up."

"I've always been strong, never negative. I really lost it today. I walked out of the meeting."

"Good for you. And maybe you can do private teaching after you give birth. You said that was an option. Not having to deal with the school rules and regulations."

"Are you auditioning for being my Mr. White Knight to rescue me?"

Warren laughed at the way Rebecca changed the meaning of his last name." Rebecca let her superiors know that she would not be returning after the Easter holiday.

"I know this is earlier than you expected for me to bail, but I need to take care of myself and my baby. The job stress is affecting my pregnancy. I hope you'll understand. If you need any help with the transition or training, I'll be more than willing to help out. I'm only a few blocks away."

On her final day, a small group of teachers took Rebecca to lunch at The Counter on Ocean Park Boulevard. A favorite build-your-own hamburger eatery that allowed the customers to creatively choose an unlimited number of toppings.

Jackie, the leader of the pack, said, "What are you going to do all day? Won't you be bored?"

Rebecca smiled when she said, "Are you kidding? I have a list of must-read books. And I'm going to learn a language. And in less than six months I'll be a mother."

"We wanted to give you a going-away gift."

The large box held a suite of maternity clothes.

Before Rebecca left, Jackie demanded, "Don't forget about us while we are killing ourselves, taking up the slack from your departure."

Walking back to Ocean Garden her nervous edges had been trimmed off and she could focus on making a beautiful child. Rebecca wanted the best parts of her DNA and Warren's to be passed on to their offspring.

Rebecca had a new project upon her return to Ocean Garden, using a bread maker to make Rosemary bread. Once completed, she had an uncontrollable urge to consume multiple slices, followed by an afternoon snooze. The nap was cut short when her stomach spasmed. Her body was talking to Rebecca but she didn't have the vitality to listen. Instead, she played an album of lullabies that would help Rebecca bond with her soon-to-be-born child. She sang along with the lyrics:

Sing your way home
At the close of the day
Drive the shadows away
Smile every mile
For wherever you roam
It will brighten your road
It will lighten your load
If you sing your way home.

Chapter 17

Client Melody

Interrupting his work on a statute deadline, Warren received a call from The LGBT Village. Melody, his pro bono client, was in juvenile hall and wanted to see him. He had promised Rebecca he would attend the weekly late afternoon Lamaze class with her, but he believed this emergency had precedence. At six months into the pregnancy, Lamaze classes were recommended.

"Rebecca, can you get Paul to go with you?"

"Yes, I can tell him he'll be auditioning for the part of the brother of a pregnant woman whose husband is too busy to go with his wife to a birthing class."

"I promise you this is the last time I'll flake out."

The light Saturday afternoon traffic to Juvenile Hall in Boyle Heights gave Warren a chance to regroup. He no longer obsessed about fatherhood. Now that Rebecca had quit her job, she would be more responsible for their offspring. He would never reveal that to Rebecca. It would make him sound misogynistic and he was anything but that. The cost of living in Ocean Garden had zoomed over the last ten years. The $550 HOA dues, along with outrageous property taxes ballooned by school bonds, severely ate into their earnings. Working only on contingency cases where insurance companies continued to squeeze settlements gave Warren a zigzagging monthly revenue. Even adding wrongful eviction cases to supplement his typical slip and falls and auto accidents didn't quite give him a competitive edge in meeting the monthly nut at the office and the townhouse. He needed that one gargantuan settlement.

He had been working with his client, Josephine. The case had the makings of a two-million-dollar payout. Warren received advice from Larry, an attorney in his office, who routinely brought cases to trial. Josephine Benson, a thirty-one-year-old fitness instructor, had been jogging in the bicycle lane in Beverly Hills when a motor vehicle driven by a seventeen-year-old boy hit her. The boy left the scene of the accident, but a witness got the license plate of the car. The jogger suffered serious injuries including traumatic brain injury (TBI) and spent three months in the hospital. The parents of the boy had a Cadillac insurance policy so the payout could be huge. Warren's gut told him that the stars were aligned towards a colossal win.

At Boyle Heights Juvenile Hall, Warren was taken to see an unrecognizable Melody. Before he connected with her in Juvenile Hall, the brightly lit walls, murals and hospital cleanliness implied faith that Melody was in a safe place. Any traces of being a female had been stripped because of Melody's crew-cut hair, cheek bruises, and red zippered scar on her forehead. Warren tried to readjust his eyes, wondering what happened to Melody's chest. Her tight white tee-shirt revealed a flat chest. The startling red bruises around her throat explained her vocal cord hoarseness.

"I am going to get killed in there. I'm beaten up every day. Last night when I was attacked, they tried to choke me to death."

"Have they told you what you've been charged with?"

"It's a bullshit charge. Assault. I'd been jumped by Benny, the school tyrant when I was walking home. Benny was Alicia's boyfriend."

Warren remembered when he saw Melody at the Village that Alicia had been involved in the bathroom incident.

Melody continued, "He started punching me. I'd learned karate to defend myself, and I proceeded to kick the shit out of him. Broke both his legs. He kept whimpering in pain and screaming at me. I ran off, but I never thought I'd be arrested. Apparently, Benny had told the police that I attacked him for no reason."

"I thought these detention centers were just temporary. Did they say how long you'd be in here?"

"No, but this is no place for someone like me. And I haven't been able to take my hormones. I can't get my prescription filled. It's fucked me up."

"What about your foster parents? Are they trying to get you out?"

"They don't give a shit about me. I think they're glad I'm here. They told the officer that I was incorrigible."

Warren wanted to separate Melody from her dog poop treatment. He regretted she had veered off his radar. That would have to be a priority in the future. Warren attempted to hug Melody but an officer stopped him.

"Warren, can you do me a favor? I'd been working for my neighbor, Mrs. Solomon. I would cook and clean after school for her. And she had the cutest kids. I would babysit. I loved doing it. Can you let her know what's going on? I don't want her to think I quit. Here's her phone number. I'm afraid to call her. I don't want her to be disappointed in me. And they only let us talk on the phone for a few minutes."

Warren's emotions were on fire from her words and told her, "I promise we'll get you out of here. And yes, I'll call Mrs. Solomon and explain what happened."

Chapter 18

Lamaze Class

During the drive to the Lamaze class with Rebecca, Paul knew D-Day was coming. As the estimated time of arrival of Paul's niece or nephew approached, he had not committed to moving in with his boyfriend, Joshua. Joshua's belabored worshiping love petrified Paul. Previously Paul's roommates had never included men called "marriage material." Paul imagined that Joshua purchased a witch's potion to get Paul to say those three magic words, *I love you.*

In four months, Warren and Rebecca would sweetly evict him. Paul's art of the deal consisted of moving out in the ninth month, giving them 30 days to convert the bedroom into a nursery. Paul would paint and set up the Babyletto 3-1 convertible crib. They insisted on environment-friendly Greenguard Gold Certified baby furniture that included a bassinet, infant dresser, and changing table.

The conversation floated to Paul's vocation. "I've decided to change course. You know I've been taking yoga classes at the LGBT Center. I'm really getting into it. I've been reading and studying on my own. So, the instructor asked me to be his assistant during class."

"I could use yoga myself. My body is going through so many changes. I didn't realize I could have so many aches. Like I'm completely out of alignment."

"The teacher runs a few studios in Santa Monica and asked me if I wanted to work for him. Just part-time and not much money. Still, it sounds like something I'd be good at. More fun than working at IHC."

"What's the name of the place? The Lamaze class is held in the Baby Yoga studio on Olympic Boulevard. Could be a coincidence that this is one of the places your yoga instructor owns."

"Oh God, yes. I'll ask him next week."

"Yes, Paul. Sounds like a good fit for you. Nothing more on the acting front?"

"No. I keep thinking I'm over 30 and still haven't gotten a break. Oh, but I have other news. I've been doing so much volunteering at the Center, and I'm always checking the job board for openings. There is this part-time job in Senior Services. Coordinating activities, lunches, and sort of being a cheerleader for LGBT Seniors. Sort of like a cruise director."

"Sounds like you're putting together a career plan."

"What about you, Rebecca? How does it feel to be a future mother?"

"Good. I wish Warren didn't put in so many hours. He works every day. And it's gotten worse since I quit teaching."

"Trying to make up for not having two incomes?"

"I don't mind budgeting. We don't have to eat out three times a week."

"Do you want me to talk to him? Brother to brother-in-law?"

"No. We'll be fine. Once money comes in when some of his cases close, it will take the pressure off."

"How's the little Knight doing?"

"The doctor said I'm doing everything right. Blood work is fine. Blood pressure is just where it should be. And the weight gain is normal. I know I hardly look like I'm pregnant."

"And what did you decide about knowing the sex of the child?"

"We were against it, but the first ultrasound that didn't announce the sex was celebrity gorgeous. Whether it's a boy or girl, they are headed for stardom."

After they arrived at the Baby Yoga studio that did double duty as a classroom for Lamaze, Paul wandered through the space to get his bearings while Rebecca visited the bathroom. Paul couldn't help gawking at the shapes of the women, carrying high or low, waddling wide or narrow hips. He imagined a baby wanting to break free and run.

Paul flirted with the idea that once he mastered yoga that he could handle teaching these classes.

The two-hour class finished, and Paul helped Rebecca rise from the floor. Her scream rattled the building. Paul held her tightly. The teacher asked, "Are you all right?"

Rebecca's face was turning colors. She moaned and tried to hold her stomach.

"It's a stabbing pain, shooting through my insides." Rebecca collapsed onto the orange pillow. There was water that surrounded the floor around Rebecca. After a pause, Paul got pummeled by an earsplitting shriek from his sister who had awakened from her faint. She slipped into unconsciousness. Another paralyzed pause before Paul shouted, "I need to take her to West Side Hospital. I think that's where her doctor practices. Can you help us to my car? I want to try to call my brother-in-law."

Rebecca went in and out of consciousness while Paul's car hustled towards WSH. He had her lay in the back seat for comfort.

He kept talking to Rebecca, "Hold on. We're almost there." Warren met them at the WSH Emergency Room at the Santa Monica campus. An attempt to reach her obstetrician before they arrived failed, but Warren was able to get in touch with Rebecca's primary care physician, Dr. Resnick. Warren insisted that her medical care involve the doctor who knew Rebecca's history. Resnick had been her physician since her teenage years.

Before the admission process began, Warren embraced Rebecca, rubbed her hands, and willed his energy force to get usurped by Rebecca. When her doctor arrived, they were able to bypass the emergency room and get her admitted to the hospital. The WSH team of physicians began to triage the patient after assessing her condition.

Warren and Paul hunkered in the waiting room gripped in a vice of emotional distress. Short spurts of sleep re-energized them to ensure they could process updated information about Rebecca's condition. Warren chewed his nails to stumps while Paul wore out his Nikes pacing the waiting room floor.

Their conversation never rose above banal. "Coffee? Did you want to take a break? Go for a walk? I wonder what is taking so long. I feel so useless."

Both of their iPhones had died lacking a charge cord. Paul offered to drive back to Ocean Garden to retrieve their chargers.

Warren said, "No, stay here. I want both of us to be around when the doctor tells us what's going on. I'm a basket case."

Finally, at two a.m., an exhausted doctor burst through the door and sat down to talk to both of them with updates. The doctor's bloodshot eyes and stringy hair foretold a gloomy forecast for Paul and Warren. When the doctor said, "I'm sorry." Paul and Warren assumed the worst, that Rebecca had died. The temporary relief they felt when the doctor said, "She lost the baby," was obliterated. He explained that Rebecca went through X-rays, ultrasounds, and a CAT scan to figure out the root of what caused the miscarriage. Emergency surgery was needed to stop excessive bleeding. Rebecca needed a D&C and there were fears that she had an underlying condition that had previously been missed.

He finished his explanation with, "She's in recovery. We'll keep Rebecca there for observation before sending her back to her room. Her body's been assaulted and she needs to rest."

"Can we see her?"

"I know it's been a long evening, but she needs to let her body heal and the best way is to sleep. So, I think it's best you come back later this morning."

"Doctor, Rebecca needs to see us. We don't want her to think she's alone. We'll just visit her for a short time and then go."

"No visitors are allowed in the recovery room. Let me check to see if she's gone back to her room."

He returned ten minutes later, smiling and refreshed. He led them down the quiet corridors through a maze of patient rooms.

Paul and Warren quietly entered Rebecca's room. Despite the darkened room, an aura hovered over their sleeping beauty. The sound of her sweet breathing brought a surge of tears to them. They stood on each side of the bed and held her hands. The warmth emanating from her fingers cried out, *don't worry about me. I'm going to be fine.* They kissed her forehead, whispered "*I love you*" and left the room.

In the hall, an embrace expressed the love they felt for Rebecca. When the volume of Warren's sobs brought a shush from the floor nurse, they quickly departed to their respective cars.

The embarrassment of exposing his frailty frightened Warren while driving back to Ocean Garden. He thought, *Why wasn't I with Rebecca when this happened? I didn't have to see Melody today. I'm selfish. Rebecca should be my number one priority. Thank God Paul was there. Does Rebecca realize she lost their child? My child. And how could I have been worried about fatherhood? And now it's not going to happen. Is something really wrong with Rebecca? Is she going to be able to get pregnant again? Fuck, Fuck, Fuck.*

Paul's car was settled in the garage when Warren arrived. The barren townhouse knew something was wrong without Rebecca. The wood floor creaked as Warren crossed the living room to climb the stairs to the second floor.

Paul's normally closed door when he was sleeping, was invitingly open. The blackened room disappointed Warren until he saw a corner nightlight revealing his sleeping brother-in-law. Warren grappled with disturbing Paul and saying goodnight. When Paul stirred beneath the blue comforter, Warren quietly mouthed, "Paul, I wanted to thank you for today."

"I'm still awake, Warren. I thought I'd be able to fall asleep from exhaustion. My mind is going a mile a minute. It's all over the map."

Warren said, "Me, too. I have too many unanswered questions. I'll need your help tomorrow."

"Of course. Anything you need. And thank you, Warren. Rebecca is lucky she has you."

Paul forced himself to wipe away the horrifying image he saw when Rebecca collapsed.

Warren verged on emotional chaos walking back to the empty king bed. He took Rebecca's pillow and pressed it to his chest, smothering his tears. A restless sleep arrived only to be disturbed by a threatening phone call at seven in the morning.

Paul and Warren attempted to revive themselves by showering and gulping down a quick and dirty breakfast. Off to the hospital.

At the hospital, both Rebecca's obstetrician, Dr. Erikson, and the primary care doctor were huddled around Rebecca's bed.

Dr. Erikson asked, "How are you feeling?"

"Like I've been hibernating. What time is it?"

"Eight in the morning."

"What happened to me? I am sore down there." She pointed to her abdomen.

Resnick held Rebecca's hand and told her, "You had a serious problem during your Lamaze class yesterday."

"My brother was with me. I don't remember anything else."

"I'm sorry, Rebecca. You had a miscarriage."

Rebecca said, "What are you talking about? I'm pregnant. There is a baby growing inside me. I know I haven't gained as much weight as you'd like. You said the fetus was perfect, no problems." Rebecca pulled her hand away from Dr. Resnick and moved her hands up and down her stomach.

"I feel my baby. Its heart is beating. Listen to it, doctor. Please, you've made a mistake."

"No, Rebecca. I'm sorry. You lost your baby. We've been trying to figure out what happened and we're going to continue to have you go through a series of tests. One thing we did find is that you have celiac disease. That was one of the reasons for the miscarriage. Also, I was reviewing your chart and the back problems you brought to my attention would also be explained by celiac disease since it's an autoimmune side effect."

Rebecca interrupted, "No, that's impossible. That's for people who can't eat gluten. I've never had a problem."

"I'm sorry, Rebecca. Celiac can be a tricky disease to diagnose because it mimics irritable bowel syndrome and lactose intolerance."

Resnick and Erickson explained the details of the surgery, what some side effects might be, and assured Rebecca that she could try to have a child again. Rebecca tried to mull over the information, still finding the events incomprehensible.

"Your husband and brother will be here soon. I can discharge you." Rebecca smiled and thought Warren and Paul would tell her that the doctors had perjured themselves. The bulge in her stomach told Rebecca she was still pregnant until the familiar heartbeat and kicking ceased. Rebecca thought, *Maybe I was never pregnant. It was a fake pregnancy. I'll pretend I had a miscarriage for Warren and Paul.*

Before they came to retrieve Rebecca from her room, Dr. Resnick gave Warren and Paul an update and told them, "I'm worried about Rebecca emotionally. She doesn't believe she lost the baby. I don't want to scare you, but she probably needs to talk this through with a therapist unless you guys are miracle workers. And I told her the minimal amount of information, I didn't want to overwhelm her with medical jargon. Her immune system is compromised and that isn't a good sign. We need to build that backup, otherwise, she'll be at risk for infections."

"What is going on with her having celiac disease?"

"Yes, we missed that. It may have been a mild case and changed. But she has to be very, very careful. It's serious. I'll email you instructions and the types of food she needs to exclude."

Rebecca sat waiting for her rescuers. Her eyes and face had a mannequin stare until she saw Warren and Paul. Her only words were, "Get me out of here." Her nurse eased Rebecca into a wheelchair, the standard discharge transportation. Rebecca refused to acknowledge Dr. Resnick when she rolled out of the room.

Rebecca remained mute during the short drive to Ocean Garden despite Warren and Paul's attempt to jabber distractions, "You know that big case I'm working on? You remember, Rebecca.

The hit and run with the jogger. It's gaining traction. It's possible there will be a settlement without a trial."

Paul followed with, "Did you make that rosemary bread from scratch? My goodness, it was like I'd gone to heaven when I took a bite. You should give up teaching and become a full-time baker." Paul regretted his words. Eating the gluten-infested bread might have triggered the miscarriage based on what the doctor said.

Rebecca entered to the smell of gardenias in the townhouse. Rebecca motioned for both Paul and Warren to join her upstairs. Without speaking she directed the three of them to lie on the king bed with Rebecca in the middle, staring at the paneled wood cathedral ceiling. The late morning heat was partially absorbed by the ceiling. Rebecca flipped on the ceiling fan to circulate the remaining simmering raw air pressing on their bodies.

Hands locked together. She searched for a way to exorcise the pain of losing her child. And as a final exorcism, Rebecca grabbed the CD of baby lullabies and let the music bounce off the walls. The lyrics took on a heartbreaking resonance.

> *"Sing your way home*
> *At the close of the day*
> *Sing your way home*
> *Drive the shadows away*
> *Smile every mile*
> *For wherever you roam*
> *It will brighten your road*
> *It will lighten your load*
> *If you sing your way home."*

After two hours, their stomachs needed nourishment. Their arousal from napping commenced with showering to remove any emotional contamination. The pounding of hot water in their respective showers allowed them to let dead skin flake off their bodies.

While they ate scrambled eggs loaded with cheddar cheese, mushrooms, onions, and chicken sausage, Rebecca said, "I've been through a horrible loss. I know there is going to be plenty of time to mourn, but today I want to make believe that nothing has changed." Warren and Paul cautiously obeyed her wishes with concern about the way Rebecca was coping. Both wanted to believe that Rebecca wasn't following the pattern of avoiding the grief she should have experienced after past losses. Paul quietly grieved over his loss of the chance to be an uncle. He had learned the damage of procrastinating mourning when their mother Edna, died.

Rebecca slowly gathered strength, and when her soreness dissipated, she acknowledged being rudderless without the structure of teaching. Jackie visited her daily and kept her abreast of the recurring traumas at school. More teachers had bailed. Funds kept getting cut. Cost of living increases were put on hold. Many of the staff were purchasing their own supplies to supplement what the district provided. Still, Jackie prompted her with, "So when are you coming back to save us? You know students and teachers and parents are always coming up to me and asking what happened to Rebecca? She was the best." Rebecca smiled and commiserated, but never answered Jackie.

The bitterness of the profession stopped her from returning to school. Paul brought her an unexpected gift when he read an article in the Los Angeles Times. It was about a deaf speech teacher, Elyse Spiker, who used the same techniques with stroke victims that she used with her young deaf students. She developed special speech therapy exercises to help patients relearn how to make sounds, form words and breathe properly during speaking. Rebecca thought if a hearing-impaired teacher could help stroke victims, that might be the kind of niche work Rebecca could do.

Rebecca Googled possibilities for a career change. Santa Monica had a private clinic specifically for stroke survivors, a bridge between hospital rehab and independent living. Rebecca began an unpaid internship at the Wilshire Clinic. They promised her once she passed the learning curve, she would qualify for hire. Rebecca learned about the different types of aphasia. Patients with Wernicke's would utter long sentences with nonsense words, while Broca's made them incapable of full sentences. The curse of Global Aphasia caused communication impairments of speaking and understanding. Rebecca took the challenge of working with elderly patients as more rewarding than working with children. Within a month she got an assignment with minimal supervision.

Her first challenge was with the local actor, Laurence Brown. Six months ago, at age 70, his stroke left him with Broca's aphasia. He was robbed of his voice, the prime instrument of an actor. She worked with Laurence three times a week to enable him to complete full sentences.

She felt like a rising phoenix, the immortal bird from Greek mythology, regenerated and arising from the ashes.

Chapter 19

Palm Springs

Paul needed a break and now that Uncle Buddy was ensconced in Palm Springs, a weekend getaway made sense. Rebecca had physically mended and Warren had cut back on his caseload to spend more healing time with his wife.

Despite Palm Springs' reputation as the gayest city in the nation, Paul had never visited the town. Joshua told him that during the Golden Age of Hollywood, the movie studios owned celebrities. For LGBT performers who had to sign morality clauses and remain within two hours of Los Angeles, Palm Springs was the perfect oasis. The fear of being outed and losing their careers had been removed. Rock Hudson, Cary Grant, and Montgomery Clift had a safe hangout.

When Paul breathed in the non-polluted air that surpassed the Santa Monica ocean breeze, he instantly relaxed. The San Bernardino and Santa Rosa mountain ranges shielded the town. The view of mountain ranges surrounding the city discharged his anxiety about career failures, the loss of Rebecca's baby and his future.

Buddy's apartment was within walking distance of the gay strip that they would explore after Paul unpacked. Buddy's apartment no longer housed an abundance of antiques. The desert furnishings stressed a Southwest sensibility. O'Keeffe framed pictures filled the walls. The turquoise earth tones on the rustic dining room chairs, sofa, and vanity table gave the home a tapestry of warmth. On the dining room table, a bouquet of twenty roses in a ceramic vase brightened the room.

"Beautiful flowers."

"It was a gift from Harry. We've been dating for months. It's gotten pretty serious."

"Good for you."

"I'm thinking about having him move in. He's a fantastic cook, too. I get lonely and having a roommate would be lovely."

"Just a roommate," Buddy laughed.

"He's way younger than me. 55 years old. Hard to keep up with him but we have done the deed." Paul enjoyed seeing his uncle happy.

"I love your place. It is so different from your place in Silverlake."

"Yes, I wanted a complete change. I felt like I was living in a museum in Los Angeles. Too much clutter and a mishmash of styles. This is so much better."

"How are you feeling? You look like you may have lost weight. Where are your love handles from Harry's cooking?"

"Very funny. I'm fine. Just feeling my age. I think adjusting to the heat has affected my appetite. Don't get me wrong. I love living here, but the heat gets intense. Thank God, I have great air conditioning. Would you like something to drink?"

Buddy offered freshly squeezed lemonade. Buddy no longer had a jaunt to his movements and the beginnings of wear and tear on his face that Paul had not noticed before, were more pronounced because of the weight loss

"How about a refill?"

"It's delicious. Yes."

Buddy took Paul's tumbler back to the kitchen. When Paul heard the crash, he found glass splattered on the red burnt kitchen floor tiles with oozing lemonade.

"Damn it. I can't believe I dropped the pitcher." Buddy had a vacant look of frustration.

"Here, let me clean this up. You're going to have a sticky floor. Don't worry about the mess, just go and sit down."

Buddy mumbled, "I am so stupid. Can't even use a pitcher. What is wrong with me?" as he retired to the living room.

Paul said, "Mission accomplished. Hey, want to go into town? You can be my tour guide."

"I'm kinda tired. Didn't sleep well last night, so I'm going to take a nap. I'll show you around after dinner."

"I need to stretch my legs so I'm going to explore the neighborhood. Maybe I'll get lucky."

Paul headed towards the main drag on Palm Canyon Drive. Even though it was May, the end of the high season because of the upcoming blistering furnace of weather, the throngs of tourists were crawling up and down the boulevard. The leftover snowbirds, a term Paul had just learned, made their presence known with international accents. Buddy had explained snowbirds. They were Canadians and Europeans who deserted their frost-bitten climates in the winter and populated the balminess of Palm Springs.

The LGBT reputation was in full force. Paul hadn't witnessed this many hot men and women walking hand in hand in Los Angeles. Paul was excited that the community integrated lesbians unlike the separation of powers in other gay meccas. Plus, the wide age gap between partners surpassed Silverlake's norms. West Hollywood and San Francisco paled in comparison. An outdoor restaurant resided between every other building. Block after block of festivities. Above the restaurants, awnings and spritzers protected the sun-worshiping patrons. The spritzers sent refreshing misting water giving the impression that fog was rolling into town.

And the smells from Las Casuelas Terraza and Copley's made Paul swoon. He could picture himself living here. The prematurely grey-haired man, barely covered with a tank top and shorts that looked more like a bikini bathing suit, kept gawking at Paul. He must be a narcissist standing against a lamppost waiting to be plucked. The Palm Springs indoctrination would be happening with an afternoon delight. Paul cruised back at him, and he said, "I'm Ed."

Uncle Buddy had a refreshed look when Paul returned in the early evening. At eight they ventured out to East Arenas Road, the gay strip of Palm Springs. The informal restaurant, Blackbook, caught their interest with a menu that boasted Nashville Hot Chicken and Street Tacos. They laughed at the cocktail selections of "Cocked and Loaded" and "Just Fuckin' Try It".

After the food arrived Paul said, "I'm worried about Rebecca. She doesn't talk about the miscarriage. Almost like it didn't happen. I learned my lesson about keeping that shit inside after Mom died. It comes back to haunt you later if you don't do some sort of grieving."

Buddy replied, "Rebecca's strong like her mom. She knows what she's doing. Privately she is mourning."

Just when the waiter gave them the check, a tall regal gentleman in a white linen blazer came toward the table. Buddy stood up and put his arms around the mystery man and kissed both his cheeks.

"Harry, this is my nephew, Paul." During the bear hug, Harry grabbed Paul's butt. Paul quickly backed away, not wanting to embarrass Buddy. He'd heard of couples having an understanding with a 20-year-old-age difference and assumed

Buddy had established that compromise. Paul might have been overthinking the playfulness. His original relief that this Harry could provide Buddy with a sexual outlet and a caretaking role, slowly dissipated.

"Hey, guys, I'm going to check out Hunters next door. I'm in a dancing mood."

Buddy said, "Go ahead. We don't want to risk our hearing."

Harry told Paul, "Nice to meet you. Maybe we can have brunch tomorrow. Buddy, do you want to stay at my place tonight? Give Paul some privacy."

"Good idea. You've got keys, Paul. We'll make a reservation for brunch in the morning."

Paul had researched Hunters, and the declaration that it was the best Dance Bar in the Coachella Valley whether you were gay or straight, made it a must-see attraction.

His afternoon diversion with Ed had ended in sexual disarray. Hunters would need to provide him with a superior grade of meat. Paul hated that he objectified men, but he had gotten into a sexual rut for the last ten years.

The scattered attendance on the dance floor reflected a bygone disco era to Paul, along with old-fashioned strobe lights. It was as though he'd taken a time travel machine to the world of the 1978 film, *Thank God It's Friday*, which took place in a discothèque. The lines from its Academy Award-winning song "Last Dance" brought bittersweet thoughts about his boyfriend, Joshua. Rather than spending the night, a butchered Paul drove to his uncle's apartment, grabbed his belongings and drove back to Santa Monica.

Joshua populated Paul's psyche during the return trip. He hated that Joshua wanted to use *I love you* to incarcerate him.

After Rebecca's miscarriage, Joshua had wanted to break Paul's spiral of depression. Both would be pampered at Beverly Hot Springs Spa in East Hollywood. The dilapidated façade of the spa made the transcendent interior astonishing. The morning encompassed the natural hot springs, followed by the cold-water plunge, and ending in the Eucalyptus steam room. The spa had reinvigorated their skin.

Back at Joshua's apartment he nervously told Paul, "I wanted to reset things between us. I know you've been devastated by not only Rebecca's loss but your loss about becoming an uncle. You are a wonderful man whom I love. And I want to share my life with you."

Paul wanted to accept Joshua's words, "First I want to thank you for today. I really needed it. And you're right it's been a rough couple of months. I know we had plans for me to move in with you."

"I've been patient and given you the time to decide."

"I know. You haven't pressured me."

Paul was unsure how to finish his thoughts. He stopped and grabbed hold of Joshua's attention by silently staring at his eyes, not straying. Incredibly difficult but he kept at it until Joshua broke the stare.

"Are you thirsty? You know I feel dehydrated from sweating out all the poisons today. Kind of draining. Why don't I make us some tea?" Joshua took the task of boiling water as a chance to avoid what Paul would be hammering at him. Paul followed him into the kitchen tugging at his waist. He cradled Joshua's head with his hands before he tried to kiss him. Joshua disentangled from Paul and said, "What are you doing? Just tell me. You don't want to move in with me. You can't say you love me. I don't care. I know you love me. Don't think just because you want to have sex that it will solve everything."

"I'm sorry. My sister needs me."

"It's bullshit. She's married and has Warren. You're just scared. You think it's some big fucking commitment if you live with me."

"I'm not scared. It's just not me. I like my freedom." A demon possessed Joshua and he wrestled Paul out of the kitchen. Hands clenched into tight white weapons. He went into road rage and then started sobbing. Paul backed towards the door, gasping at the monster he'd created wanting to annihilate him.

"Calm down, Joshua. Do you want me to lie to you? Tell you that I'll change. I don't want to be monogamous. It would kill you if you caught me cheating on you."

Joshua screamed, "Get out before I murder you."

Paul's eyes took a last gasp and pleaded with Joshua. Paul saw the relationship had been severed and he left, despondent.

Paul sat in his car and waited until the image of Joshua's knuckles that had wanted to crush him, disappeared. Paul had wished that he'd been whipped by a leather strap. On his return to Ocean Garden from Palm Springs, he couldn't stop repeating to himself, *I really fucked things up with Joshua.*

Chapter 20
Renewing Vows

At the six-month anniversary of the loss of their unborn child, Warren asked, "Do you think we should try again?"

Rebecca responded, "Try what again?"

"To have a child. Assuming you are ready to try to get pregnant."

"I'm really enjoying working with stroke patients. Can't we wait until I've been at this new job for one year?"

"I understand."

Warren had given up talking to Rebecca about the miscarriage. Warren believed that having another child might help him recuperate from his own loss. He had stuck with reduced work hours and became a model husband and lover. Despite no longer being a workaholic, his practice thrived because he'd hired Teresa, a law student from Gould's USC school, to help do research along with being a partial legal secretary. He had kept in contact with his client Melody from the LGBT center, and Warren used her to organize and manage his office. Melody's legal issues had been resolved, and she became an empowered spokesperson for transexuals.

For a conversation diversion with Rebecca, Warren proposed, "How about spending the night at our honeymoon bed and breakfast?"

"Oh, that would be wonderful. The Elizabeth, right? We could take our vows again. A new beginning. Let's go tonight." To satisfy Rebecca's spontaneity, Warren was able to notch their same suite because of a last-minute cancellation.

The late afternoon mild temperature allowed them to play in the ocean after unpacking. Warren swam around his wife and pulled at her legs recreating the scene from *Jaws* to her squeals of laughter. She tickled him in return. The waves became aggressive giving them a chance to body surf. Gliding on the surf, they elegantly traveled the imagined white caps and gently landed where the tide met the white sand.

The air turned brisk and they dried each other off quickly before jogging back to the bed and breakfast. In the shower, they used a sweet herbal body scrub on each other. The pounding hot water scraped away old skin and sand. Warren turned down the showerhead and made love to Rebecca, treating her like a virgin warrior. Queen Rebecca had marked him.

The exhaustion from the ultraviolet rays and the sexual ravishing left snoozing the only option until starvation awakened them an hour later.

Rebecca asked, "Where are we going, so I know how to dress?"

"Very casual, and it's a surprise." They both grabbed linen shorts and Hawaiian shirts.

Live music at Rosenthal's Wine Bar and Patio along with gourmet food trucks along Topanga Creek awakened their hunger and music addiction. The scent from the Vietnamese truck overpowered the other choices. Rebecca checked about gluten-free choices and the owner assured her that everything was gluten-free. They gobbled the rice paper egg rolls and then tackled pho soup composed of fish and chicken. Afterward, they agreed that it didn't compare to the cuisine they'd eaten in Vietnam, but it did the job of satisfying them.

The Anita Benson jazz trio ripped through standards. Despite the humid evening, Warren and Rebecca's goosebumps sizzled during the trio's crackling version of *"You Made Me Love You."*

They sang along with the lyrics,
You made me love you
I didn't want to do it
I didn't want to do it
You made me want you
And all the time you knew it
I guess you always knew it

On the return to the Elizabeth, Rebecca complained of gas pains, "I must have eaten too quickly."

"Did you want to stop at CVS and pick up some gas-x?"

"I'll be fine. Ginger tea sounds good. We can make a pot in the room."

The stomach pains increased and turned into sharp spasms. Rebecca kept wincing. The tea failed to relieve her ache. The fear that the truck food had been made in the same oven where particles of gluten had landed, clouded their evening. A dash to the bathroom left her heaving into the toilet bowl. When the vile smell permeated the room, Warren became afraid that he would pass out. Rebecca quickly flushed the toilet after witnessing dark blood.

Rebecca resolved, "I'm going to try to sleep it off."

Warren curled up into an endless insomnia fit of worry about Rebecca. Her moaning elicited him asking, "Do you want to go to the Emergency Room?" She whispered, "No." He checked the clock at two, three, and four. How could a perfect day end in disaster? He would insist that he join her for an emergency doctor visit.

The early morning sun burst through the slots between the brushed wood shutters. After Rebecca stirred, her condition improved but she refused breakfast not wanting to undo the healing powers of sleep. Ginger tea further settled her stomach. The bathroom mirror sent alarm bells from her blanched face during the preparation to check out of the bed and breakfast. Now, Rebecca would need to add makeup to her morning ritual.

Warren required caffeine to start functioning. After hovering over Rebecca, he began sweetly badgering her with, "Are you going to be all right? You should really call your doctor. I know it's Sunday, but she needs to know what happened."

Rebecca pushed him off and said, "Stop treating me like a child."

"Okay, I'm going down to breakfast while you're getting ready. Do you want me to bring back scones?"

"No. I'll wait until we get home before eating anything."

It was unbearable for Warren to refrain from looming over Rebecca and treating her like a fragile doll. During his walk to the breakfast nook, Warren called his assistant Teresa explaining how he wasn't sure about his schedule on Monday. He wanted her available if clients called.

During the drive back to Ocean Garden, Rebecca was quiet. She insisted they listen to KUSC, the classical music station. The melancholy Mahler's Fifth lulled them back home. At their homecoming, Rebecca told Warren, "I'm feeling much better. If you want to go to the office, it's fine. You don't need to watch over me." Rebecca enjoyed playing the role of the martyr.

A squeezed-in appointment with the doctor the following day galvanized Warren's mood. Dr. Resnick took meticulous notes while Rebecca described her symptoms. A colonoscopy and endoscopy came next. Dr. Resnick kept reassuring them, "I'm not too concerned about this incident. Could just be an allergic reaction to gluten. I'm not sure about the blood in the vomit, but the tests should answer that."

"I'm really exhausted all the time. Also, I have this gnawing pain on my right side. Is there anything you can give me for energy and to stop the pain?"

"Remember you have a somewhat compromised immune system. That is going to affect your energy level. I want to wait until we get the results before I prescribe anything. Don't want to mask an infection. Here are the instructions for the prep. It will be this Friday. That is the earliest that WSH had a slot open. You'll need to drive and pick her up, Warren."

"Yes. At your service." Rebecca didn't react to his jesting.

"What's on your mind, honey?"

"I feel awful about missing work this week. Especially Lawrence, my favorite patient. He was making amazing improvements with his speech. When I started with him, he couldn't complete a thought and now he finishes sentences."

"Do you want to stop by the clinic before we head back?"

"No, my legs feel like cement boulders. I'm embarrassed to show up. I'm not supposed to be the patient."

Warren held her hand and for a brief second her face allowed a smile. She kissed Warren's unshaven scrubby cheek and said, "I love you."

The week zoomed by and Rebecca handled the prep for the colonoscopy well. The liquid diet and laxative to clean out her intestines twenty-four hours prior to the procedure did their job. In the morning at WSH, the gastroenterologist, Dr. Elaine Furman explained to Rebecca, "We'll check for polyps and take biopsies from various parts of the intestinal wall. The same goes for the esophagus during the endoscopy. A normal procedure except for your young age. I'll talk to you directly afterward. The biopsy results will be available within a few days."

When Rebecca woke from the procedure, she asked, "Have you done the colonoscopy yet?" The nurse said, "All finished. Just rest a bit and then we'll call your husband to bring you home." Rebecca realized when her hand had been stuck intravenously with anesthesia that time had sped by. Dr. Furman's smiling face soothed Rebecca's worries when she said, "Looks good."

Rebecca had a surge of vitality during the weekend based on her gut feeling that she had passed the tests. With an infusion of energy, Rebecca was able to make a surprise visit to the clinic to see Laurence. This was the highlight of her weekend.

Monday morning after a late breakfast, she received a call from WSH. Doctor Resnick wanted to go over the results with Rebecca and that her husband should be with her. The appointment was set for Tuesday morning.

"Is something wrong?"

The nurse on the phone said, "Doctor Resnick just requested I call you and she would explain tomorrow morning."

"Thank you." The news disturbed Rebecca. A tornado twisting her insides made Rebecca collapse on the dining room chair. She had to call Warren to let him know what had transpired yet her body was paralyzed. Instead, she called Jackie for advice. Rebecca had gone with Jackie when Jackie was diagnosed with breast cancer. Jackie never got rattled. Always a cool head, Jackie had decided to have a double mastectomy because of the history of breast cancer in her family. Her supportive husband, Melvin, went along with her decision. Rebecca wanted her best friend's take.

"I just received a call about my colonoscopy and endoscopy. Instead of telling me good news on the phone, Doctor Resnick is insisting she tell us in person. This isn't good, is it?"

"Not necessarily. Maybe it was inconclusive and they want to do another test or advise you about your stomach and fatigue."

"I'm afraid to tell Warren. He's been so worried about me."

"But the doctor wants to see Warren, too."

"Yes, that really scares me."

"What about you don't tell him, and I go with you for support."

"I hate to do that. I don't like lying."

"Don't worry. You'll just tell him about the results in the evening. It's no big deal."

A wave of guilt rushed over Rebecca about this planned deceit with Jackie. She fought the impulse to tell Warren, but her cluttered brain relented to the easy choice. For a diversion, Rebecca decided to organize the kitchen. In the back of the pantry, white flour and De Cello pasta stared back at her. Artifacts from her days before she was identified as gluten-free. She grabbed the items and dumped them in the garbage. She wanted to discard the Cuisinart bread maker before a tear could escape. Could things get any more fucked up?

That evening, Warren cornered her with, "Have you heard anything from the doctor yet?"

"No. Maybe tomorrow. What's happening with your case of the century?"

"Getting closer. The other side is considering a mediation rather than a trial. We need to see what they are offering."

While they watched the first episode of the new season of *The Crown* on Netflix after dinner, Rebecca dozed. Warren cradled

Rebecca's head in his lap, enjoying her warmth and steady breathing.

He purred, "Tired baby? Wanna go upstairs? I can give you a special massage since you did such a fantastic job on my fingernails."

Rebecca responded, "I'm going to turn in. I'm planning to go back to work tomorrow and want a good night's sleep." Rebecca hated the multitude of lies. Clarity had left the room.

Jackie drove her to Doctor Resnick in the morning. Jackie rambled about the continued school traumas topped off with the increase in student class sizes. A sweet diversion for Rebecca's foggy gloom. Rebecca needed two cups of decaffeinated Peet's coffee so she could fully digest what Resnick would expound about the test outcomes. Her rebellious stomach needed to shut up. Before they arrived, Rebecca thought, *Let's skip this. Go to the beach. Why do I want to torture myself? Why didn't I bring Warren? If this is bad news, he's the only person who would be positive, and I would believe it.*

"Jackie, what if Resnick gets angry that I didn't bring Warren?"

"Stop worrying. Just tell her he was busy with a case."

Sitting in Resnick's office, Jackie held Rebecca's hand before the doctor spoke. The room cringed listening to the sound of Rebecca's nervously tapping foot.

"First, I want to tell you that this is just preliminary findings. I wanted to share this with you rather than have you worry." She had a monitor with images of Rebecca's insides. She pointed to the screen, "See this area. There are suspiciously large polyps called adenoma. We tried to remove most of them. That's what caused the bleeding. We need to watch these because they may become cancerous. You might want to get another opinion for next step options. The lining of your colon is inflamed which is another area of concern. Your esophagus is slightly irritated which is normal. We still might want to make some adjustments to your diet. I know I'm throwing a lot of information at you. Also, I'm going to refer you to an oncologist. Do you have any questions?"

Rebecca was partially relieved by the good news and not catastrophizing the bad news. "No, I'm good. Thank you, Dr. Resnick, for explaining this so clearly and being honest with me." The ominous sound of the oncologist chilled Rebecca. Rebecca slammed herself for forgetting to tell Resnick about the pain on her right side.

On the walk back to the parking lot, Rebecca looked to Jackie for consoling words, "So what do you think?"

"I'm not sure. I think you need a second opinion. I don't like the idea that they didn't remove all the polyps."

"But she said they weren't cancerous."

Rebecca's ears didn't want to absorb any of this negative talk. This had been a cluster fuck choice of bringing Jackie. Rebecca clammed up until they arrived back at Ocean Garden.

"Jackie, I'd invite you in but I'm bummed out and want to be alone the rest of the day. I also want to prepare what I'm going to tell Warren."

"Let me know if there is anything you want me to do. I can ask around for a second opinion doctor."

"Thanks for taking me. And do me a favor, don't tell the other girls about this. I mean there isn't anything to tell. I don't want a bunch of calls questioning how I'm doing. It will be enough with Warren and Paul."

Rebecca decided to roam the grounds picking birds of paradise, geraniums, and roses for the dining room vase. The character of Ocean Garden had changed from mostly seniors to an influx of pregnant millennials and children wandering the premises. Their innocent eyes leaped across the grass in search of squirrels, feral cats, and schnauzers. Rebecca thought one of those small people could have been hers.

The flower fragrance brightened the townhouse while the vitamin D from the sun took its time to revive Rebecca. Paul had insisted she reread *A Home at The End of The World* by Michael Cunningham. The last lines of the book resonated ten years ago and after today they reverberated again. After Rebecca held the book against her chest, she let her fingers travel to the last page. The waves of words spoke to her as she read about how if a person died too soon, knowing their mistakes, they would not die unfulfilled because they would be in the present and not anywhere else.

Warren would be making his grand entrance soon and Rebecca wanted to look refreshed when she documented her treacherous day. But when she glanced in the mirror, her skin had lost its spring and gave the impression of being stretched. Weight loss was the culprit because it was more pronounced on her face. The gluten-free diet had frustrated her and excluding desserts, bread and pasta took away the joy of eating and caused the loss of pounds. Rebecca's solution was to grab Bob's Organic Vanilla Ice cream from the freezer to jump-start her weight.

Rebecca bounced out of her chair when she heard the slam of the kitchen door. She saw Warren's dour face rather than his sharply defined looks.

"Where were you today? I called the clinic and they said you weren't there. Actually, I hadn't been there all day."

"I'm sorry, Warren. I went to Dr. Resnick with Jackie. I didn't want you to worry until I got news about the test."

When Rebecca attempted to hug Warren, it felt abrasive to his skin. He backed away with his arms folded, setting up a frozen wall between them.

"But I thought we were in this together, Rebecca. Why did you lie to me?"

"You've been so overprotective. At first, I loved how you were taking care of me, but now it's been too much. You look at me with those sad droopy eyes. It scares me."

Warren started defrosting and embraced Rebecca with, "Oh no, my love. I thought I was helping, but I guess I made things worse."

"I understand, but you have to give me space to tackle this on my own."

As she reported the results to Warren, he listened without reacting. At the end, he said, "You just tell me what I can do. I'm not going to push you."

"I know you have my back, and I won't be shy about asking for help. Just give me space so we can make objective decisions together."

Rebecca began her quest to steer herself towards a positive outcome. The dire second doctor's opinion led Rebecca to believe the polyps were cancerous. The operation to eradicate the polyps left her with a portion of her intestines removed to ensure the cancer had not metastasized to nearby organs. She collaborated with Warren and decided against chemo or radiation at this stage of her treatment.

Rebecca began a vigorous regimen of exercise and a strict vegan organic diet. The Santa Monica Farmer's Market in The Third Street Promenade on Wednesday and Saturday morning became a weekly religious experience. The miracle find of gluten-free sourdough bread was manna from heaven. Whole Foods provided her with anti-cancer supplements. Even with her pristine diet, Rebecca's stomach rebelled and caused nausea. Rebecca's goal of eliminating stress and stinging spasms had failed. Still, Rebecca created the illusion she was on a recovery road until her follow-up colonoscopy, CAT Scan and MRI revealed cancerous activity in her liver.

She insisted that Warren or Paul join her for oncologist visits. On the last visit, Dr. Feranski told Warren and Rebecca, "I've been humoring you about not starting chemotherapy, but if you don't begin a regimen soon, your quality of life will deteriorate."

Rebecca asked, "I'm worried that you're putting poisons into my system and it will kill my good cells."

"Things have gotten more sophisticated so that the chemo only attacks the cancer. There are a bunch of clinical trials that I can suggest. Your body is finding it difficult to fight the colon cancer because of your immune system."

Rebecca encouraged Warren to speak, "What about an alternative approach? Functional medicine?"

"I don't believe in it, but you're welcome to try. But I should warn you again that we need to take more aggressive steps."

On their drive back to Ocean Garden, Rebecca told Warren, "I was reading about this Black Witch known as Hilda. She claims she uses a form of black magic to cure people with cancer. Her practice called "Left Hand Path" has brought tons of followers to her website. There was a testimonial from a San Diego police officer with stage four leukemia. Hilda's demonic guide Astaroth cured the man."

"This sounds crazy, Rebecca."

"But how can it hurt, Warren? Nothing else is working. It's important to me, and I don't care how much it costs. I'll pay for it."

"If that's what you really want, then go ahead. But promise me if it doesn't work, you'll get into a clinical trial."

"Yes, my love. Thank you."

Her beaming smile sublimated the growing tension corrupting Warren. After he dropped her off, he called Paul, "She wants to see a witch and I told her I'd go along with it. Am I nuts, Paul?"

"Do you want me to talk to her?"

"I don't know what to do. She's so set on this. She keeps saying it's worth trying. But the cancer is spreading and she keeps postponing the inevitable."

Paul countered with, "You really think she is in denial about this?"

"Yes and no. She won't talk about how she's feeling. Keeps wanting things to be normal. Just like after she lost the baby."

"Maybe that's not such a bad thing. She wants to stay positive. After she sees this witch doctor, I'm sure she'll come to her senses."

"I hope you're right."

Rebecca got an appointment on the weekend with Hilda and recruited Jackie to drive with her to San Diego. At the halfway point in San Clemente, they walked along the surf breaks and sandstone bluffs. Jackie told her, "How is Warren handling you being sick?"

"What do you mean?"

"Have you talked about what's going to happen if you get any sicker? You know when I was diagnosed with breast cancer it brought me closer to my husband. We talked about what would happen if I died. I wanted Melvin to know how much I loved him."

Rebecca clammed up as Jackie spoke.

"Let's get going. I've had enough of this spectacular scenery."

"Rebecca, you know how much I love you. I feel like we're sisters. Don't take what I'm saying the wrong way." Rebecca remained mute until they arrived at Hilda's.

Hilda's cottage was on the outskirts of San Diego in El Cajon. Rebecca told Jackie, "I want to do this alone. The appointment is for two hours. Why don't you go check out the nearby Grossmont Mall? I can call you when I'm done." Jackie reluctantly left.

Rebecca was surprised when a poised middle-aged woman wearing a long multi-colored peasant skirt answered the door. The aroma of freshly made coffee reminded Rebecca how much caffeine had been part of her life before she began her curative diet. Hilda's welcoming smile relaxed Rebecca. She had none of the artifacts that would have identified her as a witch. Rebecca didn't see a black cauldron or witch's coven in the brightly lit dining room.

"Come in. Can I get you anything before we start?"

"No. I'm just anxious about this."

Hilda had a small doll sitting on the dining room table. She said, "I understand. Thank you for sending me your picture so I could make a voodoo doll in your image. A demonic guide is going to protect you." Hilda went into the kitchen and brought back a tray of rocks. She continued, "Now I want you to place these stones around the doll. This creates a protection vortex."

Rebecca followed the instructions.

"You know I have many students in my Pagan Demonic Guide class. They will be praying and connecting with you to destroy the cancer."

"Thank you."

"I'm going to darken the room and let the vibrations from the doll enter your body. Just relax. It takes an hour."

Rebecca dreamed of her cancer being eradicated by the voodoo doll. She kept repeating her meditation mantra to concentrate on the vibrations.

At the end of the session, Hilda asked how she was feeling. Rebecca said, "Oh God, it's a miracle. I don't have any pain."

"Good. I knew this would work. Now how are you planning to pay for this? Cash, credit card or check?"

"How much did you say this would cost?"

"Four hundred dollars. It's a little bit more than I estimated because of the student prayers."

Rebecca wrote a check from her own account. She thanked Hilda before she notified Jackie to pick her up.

Jackie asked for the details, but Rebecca said, "I don't want to talk about what happened. All I know is that it was a cathartic experience, and I feel cured. And that mysterious pain on my right side has gone away, too. I can't wait to get home and tell Paul and Warren."

That evening she told Warren, "It was amazing. I feel like I've been reborn. My stomach is good. I've got all this new energy."

Warren skeptically went along with his wife's positive outlook without being judgmental.

"Warren, I don't want to see Jackie anymore. She upset me with her negative talk. She made it seem like I was going to die and needed to get my house in order. I need positive energy around me now."

Warren's internalized tears when he hugged Rebecca brought him to a nightmarish kaleidoscope of their future.

Rebecca returned to The Wilshire Clinic to continue Laurence's progression to graduate status. Her newfound energy grounded Rebecca in an alternate reality where she was in remission. She started skipping quarterly oncology appointments. Her weight gain was further proof that she was cured.

Avoiding Jackie took lioness strength. Their over twenty-year friendship had to be severed for Rebecca's survival. Rebecca wouldn't answer her calls, texts, or emails. When Jackie made her daily house calls, Rebecca found an excuse to be at the clinic or walk her seventy-five hundred steps. In those instances when she was at home, Rebecca ignored the doorbell or incessant knocking. Jackie resorted to contacting Warren. He told her, "Jackie, I'm sorry but Rebecca is trying to take care of herself. She's in a fragile state and something you told her got her upset."

"What are you talking about, Warren? We've been friends forever. Is she mad at me?"

"She was hurt when you talked about death."

"I wanted to make sure she knew how I felt about her and how important it is to share those feelings when you have a terminal illness. That's what I did when I had breast cancer."

"I'm just telling you what Rebecca wants. You've got to obey her wishes. It's just temporary."

"Tell her I love her, Warren."

Jackie's words were enough to make Warren feel like shit.

Chapter 21

Homecoming

Two pain-free months had passed since Rebecca had visited Hilda and her successful black magic cure. The right-side ache had made a comeback in the form of gas pockets. When she had Googled the cure, turmeric and activated charcoal were prescribed. Almost instantly the ache became tolerable. This enabled Rebecca to mandate a celebration with Warren and Paul at their favorite establishment, Il Forno, on Ocean Park Boulevard. Their entrance brought, "Hey. Where have you guys been? We've missed you," from the owner, Antonio, and their favorite waiter Ernesto. Each waiter bowed to Rebecca like Dolly Levi's return to the Harmonia Gardens in the film, *Hello Dolly*. When they moved into Ocean Garden, their weekly visits turned them into local celebrities. It had been a gigantic extended family where Rebecca and Paul knew many of the customers. But their attendance had stopped when Rebecca got sick. Now Rebecca could fulfill her pledge to return to this home cooking extravaganza since her body had given the signal that she was roaring back to life. Their gluten-free menu choices cinched the deal with mixed seafood fettuccine.

Warren ordered champagne and toasted, "To my lovely, successful and prizefighting wife." Paul had written a short poem:

Rebel sister

Wrestling her life

Combating the unknown

I give her a boxful of love

Rebecca addressed the restaurant, "It's hard for me to top my husband and brother. Their love has gotten me through a shitty health year. I'm healthy now, and I knew this would be the first place I'd want to celebrate. This place means a lot to me. It's where my husband proposed to me. And we love supporting neighborhood businesses."

Warren and Paul held back a landslide of tears until the patrons stood, whooped and hollered in unison. Rebecca was a rock star.

A gallivanting night wind pushed them home. During their arm-in-arm joyous sprint, they laughed about the syrupy speeches and how they hadn't realized how important the weekly eating-out ritual had been for them. Upon their return, Rebecca's ache had reappeared. The rich food and alcohol were taking their toll on Rebecca with stomach spasms. She ingested turmeric and charcoal and felt spontaneous relief. The threesome climbed the stairs and collapsed into the master bedroom. Rebecca awkwardly said, "Paul, you know the bed is big enough for the three of us."

"Too incestuous for me but thanks for the offer."

"Oh, come on. It will be like a sleepover. Warren, what do you think?"

He giggled, "I've never slept with a man."

"You guys are crazy. I'm going to bed before we all get into trouble."

Paul scurried off like a squirrel to his bedroom. Before sleeping, he looked in the mirror and reviewed his face. Still, no acting offers. Paul bet that if he was on a criminal lineup, he would not get cherry-picked. He was heading toward professional suicide. He failed at teaching yoga. And after what happened to Rebecca at Baby Yoga, he would never be a Lamaze instructor. After vigorously flossing his teeth to shed the leftover food and crappy negative thoughts, he dumped himself into bed.

Warren and Rebecca's eight hours of entangled sleep were coming to a conclusion. Warren felt a damp sensation when he detached himself from his wife and went to the bathroom to urinate. An odd metallic smell crept up his nose when he stood at the toilet bowl. When he returned to bed, he noticed dark red blotches on the sheet. His nail-biting habit had resurfaced so that he needed to put Band-Aids on the tips of each of his fingers. Maybe he had been bleeding during the night. Had Rebecca scratched him during their devouring lovemaking? Rebecca had been a tiger preying on Warren searching for his erogenous zones. He had gladly become a passive partner while she pawed at his skin until he tingled.

But there was too much blood and when he shook Rebecca awake, she looked possessed. Her scream rattled the double pane windows when she looked down at the blood before she passed out. Warren held her limp body. Paul burst into the bedroom and when he saw Rebecca drained of color, he froze in fear.

Warren shouted, "Call 911. I think Rebecca is hemorrhaging. I don't know where all this blood is coming from."

Within ten minutes an ambulance came. Paul's brain recreated the scene from Rebecca's miscarriage when the paramedics tried lifting Rebecca from Warren's arms. The mattress was soaked with blood. Warren kept talking to a non-responsive Rebecca. He remained glued to her and refused to let the paramedics separate them.

'Sir, you need to let us take care of your wife. We need to put her on a stretcher and get her to the hospital. We're just trying to do our job."

Paul walked over to Warren and gently tried prying him away from his sister.

"Warren, let them take Rebecca. They're going to help her get better."

When the warmth of Paul's hands came in contact with Warren, he turned slack and buckled into Paul so that the EMTs were able to transport Rebecca into the ambulance.

Paul asked, "Can we go with her in the ambulance?"

"Only one family member and they'll need to sit in the front."

Warren resurfaced from his collapse, "I want to be with my wife." Warren strapped himself into the front seat while the ambulance hustled to the hospital. The roller coaster ride, complete with jolting speed bumps, made Warren grip his seat belt. Rebecca remained sleeping strapped to the crisp white stretcher despite the thunderous siren.

Halfway through the transport, Rebecca scratched the surface of consciousness. The paramedic attending to her announced, "We were able to stem the anal bleeding. I'll notify the ER before we arrive."

Upon arrival at the hospital, Dr. Feranski, Rebecca's oncologist, and Dr. Resnick were notified and after further observation in the ER, she was admitted. Tests were done to ensure she wasn't bleeding out from internal organs. She had stabilized and Resnick and Feranski concurred that Rebecca needed exploratory surgery to get to the source of the bleeding.

Warren updated Paul about the course of action, and he underwent relief that Paul would be joining him.

Five hours later the surgeon arrived in the waiting room. Warren and Paul were stripped of optimism when he stoically approached. They rose from the sticky plastic chairs they had been sitting in for most of the day.

"Please sit down while I explain what's going on with Rebecca."

The surgeon meticulously continued, "We were mainly focused on the intestines because that's where we suspected the blood was coming from. We also looked at the other organs. We found tumors in her large and small intestines along with the liver and kidneys. We couldn't remove them. We ended the surgery. Because of the damage to her intestines and to prevent further bleeding, we installed a colostomy bag. It's a small waterproof pouch that is formed between the large intestine and the abdominal wall to collect waste. This will stop any pain she might experience."

"So, what else can be done?"

"I'm afraid it's metastasized to her other organs. It's stage four cancer. We can try chemo but I'm not sure it's worth the side effects and whether it will be a promising outcome. I usually tell my patients to weigh the quality of life when making decisions about the course of action. You should discuss this with your wife when she comes out of recovery in a few hours."

After the doctor left Paul began trembling with tears when he rehashed the words that felt like daggers. Warren embraced Paul's tears and said, "Paul, why don't you go home? I can see how shaken you are and we need to put up a united front for Rebecca. Convince her that she'll be okay. I'm going to ask for a cot to spend the night. I want to be alone with Rebecca when she wakes up. You can come back tomorrow."

Paul's weeping left him drained and speechless while he untangled from Warren. The love between Paul, Warren and Rebecca had been stretched to the limit. He couldn't process that he might lose his sister. He craved for Warren to shield him. When they were clasping each other, he could feel Warren's body heat.

That evening Paul dreamed of wrestling with Warren in the sand while Rebecca was doing an ocean swim from Venice Beach. The further she swam from the shore, the more she looked like a porpoise popping in and out of the water. She had mastered the butterfly. But she had drifted away from their vision and couldn't hear Paul and Warren hollering, "Come back. Don't go so far…" The beach turned into a black and white photo of lucid clouds that turned black from the eclipsed sun.

Once ensconced in her private room, Warren watched over Rebecca like a guardian angel. Warren grabbed a chair enabling him to sit by Rebecca's bed and hold her hand. Even though she was sleeping, there were moments when she gripped his fingers like a baby wanting to be soothed by her mother. As the evening progressed, Warren found himself dozing and gradually took to the cot. He dreamed of Rebecca waking in the morning, fully refreshed and ready to annihilate the cancer beast.

Rebecca's sweet tones woke his stiff body, "Warren, are you sleeping?" Warren rubbed his eyes and attempted to stand after getting fully aligned. When he kissed Rebecca, she didn't complain about Warren's unshaven sandpapering of her face. She wanted to believe that her dragon slayer had rescued her from the demon that was eating at her insides. They communicated without speaking.

"Oh, God, what happened to me? I feel like someone attacked my body. I need to go to the bathroom. Warren, can you help me out of bed?"

Warren panicked, realizing that Rebecca was unaware of the colostomy bag.

"Hold on. Let me get the nurse. You had surgery last night."

He left the room and searched for help. Rebecca felt an unusual sensation below her waist, as though something was hanging out of her abdomen. An odd body odor embarrassed Rebecca. The urge to move her bowels overpowered her and when it passed, she worried that she'd soiled herself. Rebecca was relieved when her hands didn't find any excrement near her buttocks. Rebecca felt like she was in a different body, a profound frightening change.

Warren returned with a boisterous nurse filled with comforting determination, "Mrs. Knight, good morning. I'm going to have your husband leave the room. I want to talk to you about the new apparatus and how it works. Your doctor will be making the rounds shortly and he'll give you a more detailed explanation."

Rebecca gulped and looked at Warren in a confused state.

"Warren, what happened to me? What's going on? Tell me, please."

Warren quivered and quietly told her, "You were very sick and had surgery to stop the bleeding. The doctor will do a better job about explaining."

That damn word "explaining" that kept popping up was more shattering than any physical pain.

Finally, tearing up, Rebecca asked, "Does Paul know anything about this?"

Warren followed her lead by giving a performance showing strength while his insides felt like they were melting.

"Yes, last night the doctor talked to both of us."

"I'm mad at myself for believing that crazy witch Hilda, not seeing the oncologist sooner and stubbornly postponing chemo."

"But the doctor said it really wouldn't have mattered. It was an aggressive form of cancer. And it was your decision to not have chemo."

"We're going to beat this, but if anything happens you have to promise me, you'll take care of Paul. He isn't strong like you. We have a special bond. Remember we've lived together for most of our lives. We've talked almost every day. So, he'll need you. He doesn't have any other good friends that he's close to. So please promise me that you'll continue to let him live in Ocean Garden. That you'll shelter him."

Warren's eyes shed jagged tears, no longer keeping the façade of having a cement backbone. Rebecca grabbed Warren's hand and measuredly continued, "Now this is difficult for me to tell you. If I die and remember, that is an if, I don't want you to wallow in grief. No mourning. Celebrate my life and our love. And, when you fall in love, I would approve no matter whom you choose. You're young. You'll meet somebody. I want you to be happy." Rebecca used superhuman strength to talk to Warren. It felt like third-degree burns had blistered his skin,

Warren shrunk back and his eyes reflected the fear of hugging Rebecca so soon after her traumatic surgery and the addition of the colostomy bag.

"You can hug me. I'm not a China doll that's going to break." Their bodies had a mind of their own and knew how to embrace their love in a limitless hug.

After the restorative hug, Rebecca said, "I know we have a ton of stuff to discuss but I'm exhausted. Plus, I want the nurse to explain how this disgusting bag works. You look wrecked from sleeping on that cot. Why don't you go home and get some real sleep?"

He kissed Rebecca, told her he loved her, and as he bowed out of the room, he said, "Paul needs to hear from me and he wants to see you."

After the nurse gave her instructions, Rebecca began working on what she would tell the doctor, Warren and Paul, once she had a plan.

Warren and Paul played visiting musical chairs. Rebecca told Paul, "I know you don't want to hear about what might happen to me. I promise you I'm going to fight this thing. Still, if the cancer wins, I need you to swear that you'll take care of Warren. He's going to be devastated. He has no friends beyond work. He's isolated himself and he's going to need you."

Paul kept his drama queen reactions in check. He had done enough crying the previous evening. Because Rebecca and Paul shared the same DNA, it was difficult to imagine her being gone. Plus, Paul was thankful that his close relationship with Warren enabled him to cope.

Paul said, "Of course. I'll do anything you want; just don't think negatively. You are not going to succumb to this. Make me that promise."

Rebecca didn't respond. She wanted the freedom to make her own decisions. She wanted Paul and Warren to let her go when she gracefully surrendered. Rebecca's thoughts were interrupted by a gust of wind that hit the window.

Startled, Paul said, "My God. It's like a hurricane out there. Where did that wind come from?" The swaying palm trees were dancing wildly.

Rebecca ignored the swinging sounds. She told Paul, "I'm checking out of this zoo tomorrow and we can talk more at home. Now I need to rest. My body is talking to me so do you mind if I discharge you, my wonderful brother?"

"You love bossing me around."

Back at Ocean Garden, two disheveled men sat in the kitchen alcove silently. Paul and Warren formed a cocoon trying to insulate themselves from the fate of Rebecca.

Paul broke the quiet and said, "Rebecca seems so calm about this. Is she really that strong that she accepts that this could be terminal?"

Warren shot back, "You didn't see what she was like right after she heard the doctor. Yet she says she wants to fight."

"Has she said anything about chemo?"

"No. I'm going to try not to be judgmental. Let it be her decision."

"I should tell Uncle Buddy. He should come and visit."

For the remainder of the day, Paul and Warren took turns hovering over Rebecca at the hospital. Behind the scenes, they prepared for her discharge by stocking up at Trader Joe's. They prayed that comfort food gluten-free pasta would help regain her energy.

Her release from the hospital the following morning was celebrated by Rebecca who gave an Oscar winning performance when they wheeled her out to Warren's Lexus.

She played a recovered Elizabeth Taylor who came close to death with pneumonia and needed a tracheotomy to breathe in 1960. She'd won a sympathy Academy Award for the second-rate film *Butterfield Eight* because of her survival. Paul and Warren gasped when they saw Rebecca's illuminated life force. It was incomprehensible that she had uncontrolled cancer destroying her organs. Rebecca had been resurrected and looked so much younger than her thirty-five-year-old self that she would be carded if she tried to buy liquor.

Without any assistance, she lifted herself from the wheelchair and scooted into the front seat of the Lexus. Warren and Paul didn't have a chance to help.

Rebecca spoke first, "I can't wait to get home and eat something other than the shitty hospital food they've subjected me to."

Almost in unison Paul and Warren replied, "We've stocked up on your favorites, including a healthy dose of guilty pleasure lemon and mango sorbets along with dairy-free dark chocolate brownies."

The breezy day brought normalcy to the threesome including a viciously competitive game of Scrabble, a few episodes of *The Crown* on Netflix, and a reading session of *A Little Life*. Paul had the Kindle version while Warren and Rebecca stuck with the physical book. It became a contest as to who would finish the over 800-page novel first. The story about a gruesomely abused child, Jude, who ended up cutting himself throughout his life, was a game-changer work of art. The unflinching book chronicled Jude's heightened state of anxiety. Rebecca, Paul and Warren tried not to let the maddening and consuming character of Jude overwhelm them. The words of the novelist, Hanya Yanagihara, stuck to the ribs of Warren and Rebecca.

The author explained when things get broken and sometimes repaired, you come to understand that this damage rearranges your life to make up for your loss and could be wonderful.

The following week brought a resurgence of continued health for Rebecca and a return to the status quo for Warren and Paul. The break from serious discussion was a delicious reward. Reality could slash them in the upcoming weeks.

On Friday morning, Warren received a call from his office law clerk, Teresa, "The attorneys for the Benson case have been calling; they want to get in touch with you."

"I'll be in the office soon and will contact them. Any idea what it's about?"

"No, but whatever it is, they seemed really anxious about talking to you."

Warren couldn't stop smiling after he got off the phone.

Rebecca asked, "What is it? Good news?"

"I've got a good feeling about the case. That they don't want to go to trial."

Warren's quick-paced shave left him with a deeper than normal cut on his chin that required a Band-Aid. He rushed off to the office almost forgetting to kiss Rebecca goodbye.

Paul was headed toward a nearby directing gig. It was a non-paying job at the local community theater, Morgan Wixson. They'd gotten the rights to *P.S. Your Cat is Dead*. A perfect opportunity for Paul since he had understudied the part at the Zephyr Theater in Hollywood five years before. The comedy was about an unemployed actor, Jimmy Zoole, whose girlfriend dumped him, his cat died, and his apartment was being robbed by Vito. When Vito revealed that he was gay, an unusual relationship developed. The gay writer, James Kirkwood, teased the audience about the underlying sexuality between the men.

Rebecca didn't mind being abandoned. She needed to work on a project to get her stuff in order. That evening she would tell Warren and Paul her plans.

Midafternoon Warren called, "Guess how much they settled for?" He loved playing the guessing game with her. Which city had the coldest weather? What country had the biggest population?

"300,000 dollars?"

"Higher."

"500,000."

"Higher."

"I give up, Warren. Just tell me."

"1.5 million. And I get a third, so in a way your guess of $500,000 was correct."

An unexpected cascade of tears poured out of Rebecca. The source of her weeping was a mixture of happiness but also a regret that they wouldn't be able to enjoy the windfall together. She prayed Warren hadn't heard her sobbing.

"Warren, did you want to celebrate at Il Forno tonight?"

"No, let's save it for the weekend. I just want to spend time with you. That's enough of a reward. We'll ask Paul to make the meal of the century."

Rebecca texted Paul while he was directing and requested his culinary expertise. He returned at five with overflowing bags from Whole Foods and Trader Joe's. The refrigerator was on its way to bursting at its seams.

"Rebecca, I want this to be a surprise. Go upstairs and I'll have everything ready when Warren drags himself in. What time did he say?"

"Seven thirty, but don't count on him appearing until eight."

"Good, I've got three hours to do my magic."

Rebecca laid out a pastel light pink skirt with a sapphire blue blouse to uplift herself. She removed her colostomy bag before her shower, which the nurse had approved of. After the initial difficulty, she had mastered the art of changing the colostomy bag. With just a bit of eyeliner and lipstick, she was ready to face her men. She decided to go barefoot to switch things up since none of her shoes fit. A trip to Nordstrom would solve that problem.

Paul coordinated the dinner menu of steaming artichokes, a crispy kale salad dressed with Heirloom tomatoes, braised ahi tuna, gluten-free beer and a flourless chocolate layer cake. The mix-and-match Wedgewood china settings combined with blue floral crockery and bone china tableware were the finishing accessories for the celebratory feast.

With a half hour left he decided to call Uncle Buddy. A quick pickup with an unfamiliar voice unsettled Paul until he realized it was Buddy's friend or lover, Harry.

"Hi, it's Paul, is Buddy around?"

"He's a bit confused right now. He has good and bad days. This is the latter."

"What do you mean? Is he sick?"

"You mean he never told you? He has the beginnings of Alzheimer's."

"Oh, no! Just like my mom. Put him on the phone. I want to talk to him."

Paul waited a couple minutes, "Hi, Uncle Buddy. How are you?"

A muddled response, "Who is this?"

"Your nephew, Paul."

"Oh, I remember you. How's your mother, Edna? I haven't heard from her. She used to call me every week."

Paul's guts wanted to block this horrific news. Maybe this was a blessing that Buddy didn't have to understand how sick Rebecca was.

"Just checking up on you. I'll come out to visit you soon. Let me talk to Harry again."

Harry jumped on the line.

"Look, Paul. I'm trying to take care of your uncle. I don't know how much longer he'll be able to live here without more care. Right now, I can handle things."

"Are you sure he shouldn't be in assisted living?"

"For now, we can get by. Next time you're out in Palm Springs we can talk more about it. On days when he's cognizant, he tells me he doesn't want to go into a nursing home."

"Thank you for taking care of him, Harry. If there's anything he needs, let me know. You've got my phone number. And I'll make it a point to visit soon."

Paul pushed aside Buddy's fate and concluded dinner prep. Warren arrived miraculously on time with a bouquet of pink roses. Rebecca's descent down the stairs required trumpets announcing that Cinderella had arrived for the ball. Warren roared, "Where are your glass slippers?" at the sight of her feet. She laughed, "I'm waiting for my prince to find them."

The orgasmic food filled their bellies. Warren rambled about his windfall. Paul detailed the thrill of directing *P.S. Your Cat is Dead*. He told Warren, "I cast the straight guy, Marcus, as Vito, the gay robber; and the gay actor, William, in the play as the straight character, Jimmy.

"Interesting twist. How's that going?"

"Nice. I'm trying to make the underlying homoerotic relationship more pronounced. I asked Marcus how he felt about playing a gay character. He said, 'It's fun. A little bit scary. I've never done anything with a man, but, hey, isn't that what acting is all about?'

William said, 'Easy for me. I had to hide my sexuality when I was a teenager, so I know all about playing heterosexual.'

Rebecca said, "Get to the point. I'm looking forward to dessert."

Paul continued, "So I told them I wanted them to kiss and see how that went. I figured it would give them a point of reference for their character. They looked at me oddly, because this wasn't in the script. Marcus looked ready to jump ship until I told him this isn't about you. It's the robber, Vito. He doesn't even realize he's attracted to Jimmy."

Warren, "So did they kiss?"

"Yes, in fact, it was a really long kiss. I don't know if they were playing with me or really getting into it. I had to stop them."

Warren and Rebecca laughed. Warren thought to himself what it would be like to sleep with a man. He'd never been curious about the male body even if Warren could detect the aura of a good-looking man. He despised men that were cognizant of their beauty and used it as a power play to influence both men and women. Thank goodness he had outgrown his narcissism in college. He had a strong sense of his own sexuality and a man would be of no interest to him sexually.

Rebecca mused about her planned return to the Wilshire Clinic. She revealed that the school district offered an alternative to teaching. She would evaluate speech teachers and their analysis reports of students. Rebecca said, "I love it that I won't be subjected to the stress of parents and the student load. Jackie convinced administration that I could do it from home."

"Oh good, you're talking to Jackie again."

"Yes, we had reconciled after we had a crying session admitting we were both pig-headed."

At ten Paul announced, "Hey, guys. I've got a date. I know it's late but we've been trying to hook up for weeks. I plan to spend the night. I love you both." Warren and Rebecca profusely thanked him for the dinner.

The evening closed with Warren and Rebecca savoring each other, better than makeup sex. This was the first time they made love since Rebecca had a colostomy bag. They had had an intimate conversation about what would work and sexual positions that would make intercourse not only pleasurable for both but anxiety-free. Warren kept checking in with Rebecca, and her moans of ecstasy wordlessly answered his question.

"Are you sure you're ready for this, Rebecca?"

"Yes. Hug me and go slowly. Don't worry about me." Rebecca and Warren hypnotized each other with their body movements and their skin was ready to enchant their lovemaking.

Warren couldn't tell where his body ended and Rebecca's began.

"I'm lost in you, Warren."

Afterward, they stared at the cathedral ceiling and let their temperature return to normal. Rebecca said, "I would love to go to Paris. We've never been."

"Of course. And we would do it right. Get first-class tickets not like the coach section when we went to Vietnam. Go high-end with five-star hotels."

They drifted asleep with images of the Paris bucket list that had them on a scavenger hunt for the best of the twenty areas or arrondissements.

Rebecca didn't regret not informing Paul and Warren about the big decision she'd made. There was time for that.

Warren, being a morning person, rose earlier than Rebecca, kissed her goodbye with, "I love you," and traipsed off to the office. Rebecca languished in bed. Her feet ached and appeared swollen. Thankfully, she had a follow-up appointment with the oncologist in the afternoon. It had been two weeks since she'd been hospitalized.

Rebecca was influenced by the soft weather to eat breakfast on the patio. She spread the *Los Angeles Times* on the green steel table with her decaffeinated Peet's coffee perched in her *My Favorite Wife* mug. Having coffee instantly brewed was the beauty of the Keurig. She refrained from any other breakfast because her sore feet tingled and burned when she walked or stood. While she read, the sun caressed her tight feet. She drifted off daydreaming about last night and Paris.

Paul dragged himself back to Ocean Garden at noon. His Grindr date from last night with Benjamin left his batteries depleted. Between directing, whipping together the celebratory dinner, and light S&M playing with Benjamin, Paul looked forward to downtime with Rebecca. She had mentioned a shopping spree for shoes. A lazy afternoon at the Santa Monica Mall with his sister was an easy revitalizer.

Paul saw the back of a static Rebecca sitting in the atrium when he shouted, "Hey, Rebecca, want to grab some lunch? I'm starving." Upon closer inspection Paul found his tranquil sister looking ready for a painter to do her portrait. The sun reflected off her powerhouse features but her mysteriously closed eyes would be a challenge for an artist to capture her essence. Paul proceeded to wake Rebecca with a nudge. When her head fell to the table, Paul screamed. Ocean Garden wept.

The doctors determined that the combination of the cancer spread and swollen legs caused by edema put a strain on her heart. The death certificate reflected heart failure as the reason for her death. Warren and Paul were on illogical speed dialing of busyness to avoid grief. Cremation came first. The dull pain prevented them from giving any directions to the Neptune Society regarding how Rebecca's ashes should be scattered. As a default, they were told, "We take the ashes and drop them in the ocean for the family." Warren resorted to chewing the flesh around his fingernails, enabling the swollen red digits to be oozing pus. He stopped bandaging the infected fingernails, making them visible to the throngs and able to divert the stabbing pain of Rebecca's death. The lyrics from the song they'd danced to at their wedding bludgeoned him, "In Whatever Time We Have."

Notifying friends and relatives became step two. Warren had Jackie spread the news at school and the Wilshire Clinic. Each Ocean Garden resident attended the memorial service. Their neighbors Alexandra and Garth coordinated the event to be held seven days later in the recreation room. Harry drove in from Palm Springs with a tear-stained Buddy for the service. Paul's ex Joshua made an uncomfortable appearance. Their embrace burned Paul with memories of their last brutal encounter. A few of Warren's work cohorts were in attendance along with his office manager, Melody, and law clerk, Teresa. Warren and Paul didn't speak during the ceremony, sitting numbly while the parade of Rebecca's friends spoke. The shock of her death at thirty-five continued to slash Paul and Warren. No voice to scream. During the period after the funeral, Warren became emotionally stagnant while Paul used his sex addiction to self-medicate with multiple Grindr hookups. For the week after Rebecca's death, Ocean Garden delivered sustenance for Paul and Warren. Ocean Garden's energy rippled through Paul and Warren to quiet their mourning.

With only a seven-day interruption, Warren returned to his office. Warren only used the townhouse for sleeping, a device to limit any memories of Rebecca. And for sleeping, he perched himself on the living room couch. If he attempted to sleep in their upstairs bedroom, it felt like an avalanche of bricks was crushing him.

Warren's face creased when he entered his office, ignoring his staff, Melody and Teresa, before he walked into his private sanctuary. A blue glass vase of daffodils brightened his wood desk, with a sympathy note from Melody and Teresa. An attempt to cheer up their returning defeated warrior.

The desk was littered with paperwork and mail organized by Melody as to their importance. Open cases were in one pile, invoices for office expenditures in another, and uncategorized items in the third stack. A letter from the Benson case was sitting dead center on his desk. Warren used a sharp letter opener and stared at the contents. He sneered at the check for 1.5 million dollars. This should be shared with Rebecca.

His diseased fingers wanted to rip the check in half. Instead, Warren grabbed the vase and threw it against the wall. The explosion brought Teresa and Melody into Warren's office, but before they could ask what was wrong, he screamed, "Get the fuck out. Leave me alone." Warren's screeching tears and wailing turned his eyes into red blotches and his throat raw. He collapsed on the floor searching for shards of glass to carve holes into his legs. He understood the self-medicating cutting that Jude performed in *A Little Life*. Warren's love for Rebecca had been stretched off-kilter by her death. He'd failed to make time elastic to stop him from snapping. He lay on the floor waiting until his emotional purge ended. He kept thinking, why was the love for Rebecca hammering bullets into my chest? Shouldn't I be glad that I loved her rather than wishing I'd never fallen under her spell?

Warren's recovery included an apology to Teresa and Melody. He roared through his paperwork and updated his calendar for cases nearing their statute of limitation dates. The day evolved into the early evening. A mysterious itch in his genitals made him travel to the bathroom for inspection. He'd heard of jock itch but had never experienced that sensation. After his penis passed a visual test for a culprit, he proceeded to check the testicles. A pimple with reddish eruptions was exposed…the source of his itch. He Googled for an answer and recognized the diagnosis of herpes. Had Rebecca come back to haunt him? A doctor would need to confirm before he self-diagnosed the acyclovir that Rebecca had used when she had had a breakout.

Chapter 22
Paul Regrets

Paul wanted to recreate his own version of *cutting* with Benjamin, his Grindr fuck buddy. Since Rebecca died, he had spent most nights at Benjamin's studio in Venice. Ben was an efficient passive partner, quiet but intense. No conversation. Paul immediately stripped after his entrance and prodded Ben into the corner with his fists. Paul needed Ben to be the aggressor. He rambled, "Slap me, Ben. Make me scream. Rip my insides." Paul prayed that Ben would damage him but Ben's squinched-up face reflected cluelessness about role-playing. A disgusted Paul left midstream during the sex act. His anger subsided with an iPhone ringing. William Garvey, the actor playing Jimmy Zoole from *P.S. Your Cat is Dead*, said, "Hey, when is the next rehearsal? Look, aren't we opening in two weeks? I'm sorry about your sister and you're grieving, but please don't abandon us."

His directing duties at the Morgan Wixson theater hadn't worked as a diversion from the thrashing of Rebecca's death. Still, William's pleading gave Paul an idea.

"I'll email everyone and let them know we'll restart tomorrow. I know it's late but I'm really in a shitty place. Feeling lonely. Could we meet for a drink at The Bird Cage on Main?"

"Sure. Give me a half hour to get ready and I'll meet you there."

The Bird Cage on Main Street was a recently opened bar that had the notoriety of being the only gay watering hole in Santa Monica. Situated on the top floor of the chic restaurant, The Victorian, The Bird Cage had a speakeasy dive décor that Paul called his neighborhood bar. Named after the film *The Bird Cage* where a gay Miami drag club owner pretends to be straight and hides his relationship with the flamboyant star of the club for the sake of their son who wants to marry. Rebecca and Paul had worn out their VCR tape of the movie because of Nathan Lane and Robin Williams' pitch-perfect hysterical performances. The last viewing brought an unusual comment by Rebecca, "You know even though the film is a ridiculous farce, I love the parenting skills of Lane and Williams. They make great fathers compared to many of the straight parents I see at school. Talk about unconditional love to ensure their son's happiness. You'd make a wonderful father, Paul." Paul never considered himself marriage material let alone a parent. He wondered what Rebecca had seen in him to make that observation.

Paul situated himself in a corner chair, giving him a chance to wallow in Rebecca's death. She had wreaked havoc on Paul's verve. The lack of daily conversations with Rebecca had left him mutilated. When Paul tried talking to an invisible Rebecca it felt disingenuous. Chatting to himself failed to duplicate Rebecca's interaction. Rebecca had become his amputated Siamese twin. For thirty-four years since he was born, they'd only physically been separated for those years between Rebecca's residence in Ocean Park and the beginning years at Ocean Garden. Without the daily *"I love you"* declaration with his sister, he'd fallen into an earthquake fissure. The ground had cracked open and swallowed Paul.

The Monday night barren space didn't percolate until William's boisterous narcissist actor personality arrived. William's six feet towered over Paul. The perfect vessel to lift Paul from his gloom. William became a willing subject following their consumption of two Corona beers. Paul insisted, "Can we go back to your place and play? I need someone to sexually gouge me." William clawed at Paul's body and hauled him off to his apartment.

Directing William in *P.S. Your Cat is Dead* had been joyous. William never questioned Paul about directing choices. And the ease with which William made straight actor Marcus, who played Vito, comfortable during their kissing session, gave an underlying gravitas to the entire production.

At William's miniature studio apartment in Venice, Paul gave him measured clues about what he expected sexually. A role-playing textbook S&M scene. William tied Paul to a metal kitchen chair with thick rope, like the way his character was immobilized in the play. Handcuffs tied to the chair made his hands useless. The finishing touch of gagging Paul with a thick white sock took him to an erogenous pain-inflicting zone.

Paul said, "Hit me so hard that I cry." William slapped Paul's face with such force it felt like Paul's teeth had been dislodged. Paul didn't flinch, expecting further torture. William used his tongue to lick and pull against Paul's hairy chest. The combination of agony and pleasure worked Paul into a freefalling state he'd prayed for. William surveyed Paul's dilated eyes for a red light.

"Have you had enough punishment, you bad, bad boy?"

Paul shook his head. William licked and nibbled on Paul's fingers like the cleanup from barbecued ribs. William graduated to biting. He started with fingers and then traveled along Paul's contour, leaving red teeth marks.

Paul's writhing clued William that he'd gone too far. Once Paul was untied and ungagged, his face turned serene. He thanked a disappointed William who assumed this was foreplay leading to orgasm, but Paul left.

This started the process of extricating himself from the grief of Rebecca's death and his obsession with a failed career. He regretted never using the words *"I love you"* with anyone but his sister. Soon, he'd want to speak with Warren about their shared mourning. He contemplated how Warren would react if he used those horrifying words, *I love you* to cement their brother-in-law status. Could that break the recurring tapes of remorse? Warren was a bridge to the essence of Rebecca. With Rebecca gone, Warren became his closest emotional ally.

Chapter 23

An Alternate Universe

Warren's doctor appointment had begun with Doctor Levy lambasting him after witnessing his mutilated fingers, "What have you done to your fingers? They look infected. I'm going to prescribe antibiotics. God, I've never seen such a bad case of nail-biting. Have you thought about therapy or hypnosis?"

"That's not the reason I'm here. I've got this weird thing on my shaft. I'm worried that it's herpes. It itches and stings."

Warren dropped his pants and Doctor Leavy confirmed that it was in fact herpes. A prescription for acyclovir would solve that problem.

"Did I pick this up from Rebecca?"

"It's possible. Stress is another trigger. When was the last time you had sex with your wife?"

"She died a month ago of cancer."

"I'm sorry. She was pretty young. And here I am complaining about your hands. My heart goes out to you. If there is anything you need, let me know. I can prescribe pills to help with depression or sleep."

"No, I'm okay. Thanks for the prescriptions, and I'll try to stop the nail biting. Seems like every time I give it up, something goes wrong. This is the first time I've gone off the wagon since Rebecca's miscarriage. I've got to get back to the office."

"Take care, Warren."

Warren left shell-shocked. Explaining Rebecca's death to Doctor Levy felt like a scalpel digging into his heart causing him to remain paralyzed in his Lexus.

Once Warren picked up his prescriptions at the Rite Aid on Pico, his stamina resumed enough for him to return to his office. He swallowed both pills and imagined instantaneous results. He worked until nine that evening on a new accident case involving three cars. The complexity of dealing with multiple clients was a welcome challenge. Teresa had met with the client, and Melody set up a colored folder to handle the case. Between Teresa and Melody, the office ran like a sweetly oiled machine. He texted Paul, *I'll be very late tonight.* Paul had continued to prepare dinners that were easy for Warren to reheat. After he pried himself away from work, he dragged himself back to Ocean Garden at ten. He gulped the turkey loaf with veggie Spanish rice that Paul left and prepared for bed. The ache in his back told him that he couldn't continue sleeping on the couch. He had to face their king bed and sleep there for the first time since Rebecca's death. He entered the bedroom with the lights off, enabling him to plunge into the king bed without having to witness the cavern Rebecca left in the mattress. Warren's exhaustion helped him crash to sleep. And knowing that Paul was in the other bedroom gave Warren a reprieve from the aching loss to let him sleep through the night.

The following morning Warren told Paul, "You know I can't imagine living here alone without you. You remind me so much of your sister. You try to keep me sane and you're a great cook, too. Thank you."

Paul had an urge to tell Warren *I love you* but his phobia about those three words endured. As a substitute, he lifted Warren from the sofa and infused him with the warmth of his arms in an excessive hug. A moat surrounded them to capture their vulnerable eyes.

Warren became an empty vessel and wanted Paul to possess him. He let Paul's animalistic smell which reminded him of Rebecca tug at him until Warren experienced confusion during the hug. As though he'd awakened after being in a coma and was adjusting to a new reality. He had acquired an unrecognizable sensation hugging Paul. He had to break away before Paul overwhelmed him. And the way their eyes made contact, frightened Warren as if Paul were sneaking a look into Warren's thoughts. He recalled the pledge he made to Rebecca about being a guardian angel for Paul, and yet Paul was nurturing him.

They were dissolving into extreme emotionality until fear made Warren back away.

"Warren, what would you think about going back to Venice Beach for volleyball? It's been ages. See if we can keep up with millennials."

Warren stopped looking at Paul and said, "I would feel guilty having fun so soon after Rebecca died. I'm just not in the mood."

"Do you really want to mope around all day? How about we just go for a short time? If you aren't enjoying yourself, we'll come back here or go to brunch on Abbot Kinney. There is a new place I'm dying to try out. You could use the extra calories."

Warren's eyes remained focused on the floor; he couldn't handle Paul's staring.

"Okay. How about we take separate cars if I want to be a party pooper?

Three hours of whacking the ball with tattooed boys and baking in the sun left them spent. Paul remembered he had directing duties with the play opening in a week. Warren had a "to-do list" at the office. They both pretended that the rollercoaster alternate universe earlier that morning was a fond memory and that their lives would return to an old normal rather than a new one.

Warren attended the opening night of *P.S. Your Cat is Dead* the following Saturday. Teresa and Melody had turned down his offer so he was solo. The theater buzz lifted the evening at the three hundred-seat venue which the program said was the oldest established theatrical institution in Santa Monica, founded in 1946. A sweet embellishment in the program had Paul's biography that said he was dedicating the play to his sister, Rebecca, who had recently died. She was his biggest fan.

As the play progressed, Warren was intrigued that the straight character, Jimmy, almost enjoyed being tied up by Vito, the gay thief. The back story of Vito having a wife that left him when she found out he was gay puzzled Warren. He couldn't imagine marrying a woman if he was gay. Paul had found a way to bring out the eroticism between Jimmy and Vito so the ending where they are in bed was believable. Warren loved when Jimmy had the line, "I wonder, does everything have to make sense? I wonder. Even in the real world as opposed to now, when things make sense, they really don't make sense."

Paul had asked Warren if he wanted to stay for the opening night party, but he declined. Let Paul bask in the glow of his success that was confirmed by a standing ovation. During Warren's walk back he mused about his feelings for Paul. He wondered if he was experiencing a kind of transference from Paul to Rebecca. Each time Warren emotionally thought about Paul, a jolt of fear racked him so he used a deadbolt to make it remain impenetrable in his brain.

Chapter 24
Coming Out

For three months, Warren was cursed with insomnia. On Bastille Day he lay in bed alternately gazing at the twirling overhead fan then switching to the clock showing midnight. Unfortunately, the full moon made those objects visible. The unusually humid July air was seeping through the open glass sliding doors to the balcony off the master bedroom. The rumbling compressor from air conditioners coming from the north and south townhouses prevented Warren from falling asleep. He blamed the climate change impact on Santa Monica that had brought about the need for air conditioning. Another in a list of projects Warren had procrastinated on. The wide-open windows accentuated the sound of squirrels scurrying along the roof. A noisy catfight brought Warren to the brink of sleepless insanity.

Warren was glad when he heard the creaking feet on the stairs which signified Paul had returned from his latest escapade. At times Warren felt like a parent waiting for his teenager to return. This evening Paul did not enter his own bedroom, he came into Warren's. Was Paul drunk? Did he want to talk? Paul had a fetching quality that constituted a growing list of characteristics reminding him of Rebecca. The same perky ears and unblemished long fingers with smooth, unpitted fingernails, unlike Warren's maimed digits.

"Paul, are you okay?"

"No, I wanted to talk, but you're trying to sleep. We can chat in the morning."

"I'm wide awake. Tell me what's going on. Grab a chair and talk."

The full moon tricked Warren into imagining it was Rebecca. Paul moved like his sister, a quizzical cat. Paul would use his hand to flip his wavy hair off his forehead, a copy job from his sister. And if Warren closed his eyes, he heard the timbre of Rebecca's voice. A musical lilt where she modulated words with perfect clarity. That's what made her an exceptional speech therapist.

"I'm just tired of sex. I'm in a rut. Every guy I meet is the same. They are gym rats, go to the Sunday beer busts at The Motherlode in West Hollywood, and want to fall in love and get married."

"Poor Paul. I never did figure out why you never had a steady boyfriend."

"I guess I have intimacy issues. I've never told anyone, 'I love you'... well, except Rebecca and, of course, that wasn't sexual."

"But you're unhappy. What about Joshua? You almost moved in with him."

"He wanted me to be monogamous and tell him I loved him. When I tried to explain my issues, he had a fit. We broke up."

"So, there's been no one you've come close to falling in love with? I can't believe that."

"Warren, this chair is so uncomfortable, it's killing my back. The bed looks so cozy with all those pillows. Is it okay if I sit on the other end?"

"Sure. Behave yourself. Just don't think I'm going to change to your team."

They both nervously laughed, suppressing an underlying tension. Paul looked at Warren and said, "You know we'd met a long time ago when I was in the seventh grade at Bancroft. I was watching you run. I took you to an old, abandoned house on Formosa. There was something going on between us until a rat scared us off."

"Oh, my god. I knew you looked familiar, and I couldn't place it. Why didn't you say anything?"

"I don't know. You know, I didn't figure it out until your wedding. I thought it would be uncomfortable to bring it up. Plus, I didn't want Rebecca to think I'd almost had sex with her husband."

"But nothing happened, right?"

"True, but I wanted to. I'd never seen anyone so handsome, assured of themselves, and you seemed to be interested in me. Remember, you let me watch you when you were showering."

Warren nervously laughed and said, "Oh God. I was so full of myself in those days. A conceited brat. Thank God, I outgrew that. How come we never met up again?"

"You went to Fairfax and I was at Hollywood High. Warren, am I putting you to sleep?"

Paul looked at his sleeping brother-in-law. His mind went into overdrive thinking he was the kind of man he could fall in love with and maybe try to be monogamous. He could easily say, *I love you* to Warren. Paul envisioned a genie granting him a crazy wish that would make Warren gay. He'd never had sex with a straight man and didn't want to try with his brother-in-law. It felt incestuous and dishonoring of Rebecca. Still, Paul felt cushioned by being in bed with Warren. He took off his shirt and pants, leaving his underwear and tee-shirt on despite the hellish temperature, turned away from Warren, and went to sleep.

Warren was disoriented, feeling the warmth of Paul next to him while a welcome breeze swirled. Since Rebecca's death, any physical contact from a brush, a handshake, or a hug with Paul caused an uncomfortable prickle. The first time he'd experienced not waking up alone since Rebecca had died five months before. Warren wondered why Paul was in his bed until he remembered the conversation with Paul the night before which must have morphed into a sleep potion for both of them. Paul continued to sleep in the fetal position which reminded Warren of how Rebecca would cuddle up to him. Paul's tan arms and bleached curly chest hair peeking through his white tee-shirt gave Warren a melancholy aura. Warren almost kissed Paul's forehead, as though he was Rebecca. Warren was diving into uncharted shark-infested waters, with these irrational thoughts about Paul. Where were they coming from? He quickly left the bedroom and showered off those dangerous thoughts. The story about their first encounter in junior high haunted Warren. What was going on in his head? He'd never questioned his sexuality. From the time he'd started masturbating, he'd always thought about women. Yet, according to Paul, he'd been flirting. And what about those years in college when he'd spend hours in front of the mirror, checking out his face. What was he looking for? Was he a narcissist? He couldn't decipher what it was about the image of Paul that guaranteed refuge. Not that he was a replica of Rebecca, but that Warren saw himself in Paul's eyes.

Warren made a fresh fruit salad with Greek yogurt for breakfast and when he finished his first cup of coffee, Paul appeared.

"I had such a great sleep. It was wild. You were okay that I slept in your bed?"

"I was so tired and glad that I could finally fall asleep that I didn't care who was in bed with me. It was nice not having to wake up alone."

Paul had no response. Had there been an outrageous turn of events where Warren wanted to take this relationship to another level. Paul felt ambushed and fell back into his walled-in emotional pattern. He changed subjects with, "I'm thinking of getting a teaching assignment at Santa Monica College. Maybe start with adult education then work myself into teaching drama. It would be good for me to get out of my rut."

"Excellent. What ever happened with other directing jobs? Didn't you get any traction from *P.S. Your Cat is Dead?*"

"No, it's considered community theater. Hardly ever gets reviewed except in throwaway newspapers. It's perceived as second-class work even though it can stand up to any theater in town. I'm fed up with going to auditions and working at IHC." Paul couldn't stop looking at Warren. He was falling into a chasm of love for this man and needed to exit before he did something he would regret.

Warren asked, "Do you have any plans for this evening?"

"No, nothing special. Might go to the Westside Pavilion to see a film."

"If you're not going on a date, could I join you?"

What was going on with Warren? Was this some sexual meteor hurtling toward the two of them? Paul had no choice but to answer, "Yes, but I'm picking the movie. The WW2 war film, *Dunkirk.*"

Paul and Warren were gripped by the visual dynamics on the screen that told the true story of a mission that ended up saving 330,000 French, British, Belgian and Dutch soldiers on Dunkirk Beach. Their fragile egos sniffled at the finale. Both were suckers for male camaraderie.

Back at the townhouse, Warren asked, "You know, Rebecca used to help me with my fingernails. Soaking and massaging them, sort of like a manicure. It's difficult to cut my nails, especially on my right hand. Would you mind doing this for me? I keep trying to stop chewing my nails without success. And they ache all day."

Paul was game and took a large ceramic bowl from the cupboard and filled it with warm water and a mixture of zesty lemon, rose, lavender oils and lotion. Paul said, "Do you want to remove the bandages on your fingertips?"

"No, they'll fall off once you've soaked them."

Paul took Warren's large rough hands and gently placed them in the bowl. He began massaging the palms, searching for pressure points. Then Paul cupped his hands like a fist and rolled his open fist up and down Warren's fingers. Paul had a hidden talent for massage and manicures. The bandages fell off just as Warren had predicted. Paul rubbed Warren's swollen knuckles until they began shrinking. When Paul focused on the raw tips of Warren's fingers to loosen the skin and nails, Warren winced.

"Am I hurting you?"

"No, you're doing it correctly. No pain, no gain."

Paul was buffing out the scar tissue in the finger joints. Each of Paul's maneuvers created an electrical current between them. Not sexual. The aroma and the grip of Paul's hands brought an unfamiliar sensuality. Paul asked, "Why don't you take off your wedding ring? You probably have dry skin under there."

"I've never taken off the ring since we got married."

"Just for a minute. I promise we'll put it back on."

When Paul removed his wedding ring, Warren plunged into a moment of liberation until he pivoted to stabbing guilt. Only five months since Rebecca had died. What right did he have to feel this? He couldn't even quantify what he was feeling with Paul.

Then Paul clipped Warren's nails, cleaned the raw peeling skin, and trimmed his cuticles. Warren's hands had been transformed from ugly maimed digits into close to normal. Paul hoped this fresh start for Warren's fingers would prevent the self-mutilation of his fingers in the future.

"You're a miracle worker. Almost as good as your sister."

"It is amazing… the change. Good enough for a commercial. Now don't let my work go to waste by biting your nails."

Warren said, "How much do you charge?"

"How about we do a trade? Wanna give me a pedicure? My toes are in almost as bad shape as your fingernails."

Warren acquiesced, not wanting the insane fantasy to end. When Paul removed his socks, Warren did not notice any serious damage, Paul must have been exaggerating. Warren sat on a stepstool and began massaging Paul's toes.

Paul cried out, "I'm ticklish. Stop."

Warren said, "Don't be a baby. I'm just getting started." Warren used his knuckles and kneaded them against Paul's feet. Rebecca had told him it felt like she was having an orgasm when Warren performed a pedicure on her delicate feet.

After he dried Paul's feet, he took a special jasmine moisturizer and rubbed his feet.

Paul stood and observed Warren's work, "Boy, you are good. I can see why Rebecca fell in love with you. Wow!"

Just as Warren moved the stepstool away and he tried to stand, he lost his footing and collapsed into Paul.

"Careful, Warren." When Warren plugged his body into Paul, he wanted time to freeze. The power of Rebecca through Paul was galvanizing Warren.

"Warren, what's going on? Do you know what you're doing? I'm your brother-in-law." Warren refused to hear Paul, instead he cupped his hands around Paul's angular face. He stared into Paul's quizzical eyes and saw himself and Rebecca. He was on a mission to wipe out the pain of losing Rebecca. He didn't know if he could make love to Paul. It didn't matter. He loved Paul, and he knew that Paul loved him. If he progressed, he wouldn't be able to take a time machine back to his previous life.

Paul's gut said this was wrong but he had zero resistance to Warren. He didn't doubt that Warren was straight, so it didn't make sense. What would Rebecca think if he had converted Warren into a gay man? His friends would joke about straight men with gay sensibilities and say that *he could be had*. But not Warren. Maybe he just wants to experiment. He missed Rebecca and thought Paul could replace her. Sounded like the plot of the Hitchcock film, *Vertigo,* or her namesake, *Rebecca.*

When Warren said, "Let's go upstairs." Paul melted.

As they climbed the steps Warren was basking in the smoothness of his hands. The fingernail pain had subsided. And holding Paul's hand gave his engine a jump-start. Before they entered the master bedroom, Warren realized something was very wrong. His left hand felt naked. He started heaving and spat out, "Where is my wedding ring, Paul? You said you'd put it back on."

"It must be in the kitchen. I'll run and get it."

Warren was paralyzed until Paul returned with the ring and said, "It's a sign from Rebecca. She wants me to grieve. I don't deserve any happiness. I don't deserve you, Paul. I can't do this." Warren's attorney's mind had been shut off, no longer worrying about the words he used, whether they made sense or not. Were they honest or were they just mindless chatter?

Paul took Warren's hand and slipped the ring on his finger. Warren's ring finger no longer felt unnatural.

"Rebecca would have approved."

Paul inched closer to Warren and began using his lips to intoxicate him. Rebecca was haunting him through Paul. The shock of Paul's unshaven face bristled against Warren with a force field of masculinity. Warren was both terrified and relishing the first time he would make love to a man. When Warren's hands instinctively found Paul's erogenous zones, his body surged. Paul's hips were playing with Warren. Paul's furry legs electrified Warren's hairless legs. Paul reciprocated with the precision of a car detailing, leaving Warren sexually tickled. Paul was a patient teacher. If he sensed any hesitation on Warren's part, he stopped. The recognizable facets of the male torso hypnotized Warren. It provided the safety net of letting Paul invade him. While Warren was making love, the image of Rebecca flickered like an old silent film, guiding him with compassion. After they both reached orgasm, they remained glued together in bed for the entire night. Their second night of unencumbered sleep since Rebecca died.

Beginning the following morning, they entered into a honeymoon arrangement. They were able to pulverize the gut-wrenching loss of Rebecca and replace it with their sheltering love. Rarely leaving Ocean Garden except for Warren's work and Paul's new teaching endeavor at Santa Monica College. They were bears, hibernating in their Ocean Garden den waiting until reality returned.

The walls of their world had narrowed because they were unclear on how to present this new relationship to the world. They remained cloistered, unable to explain Warren's conversion to bisexuality and the transformation of brothers-in-law to lovers. How would it appear to Jackie, Teresa, Melody and Uncle Buddy, when Rebecca had only been dead five months? But they were running out of time because Thanksgiving would arrive in two months and they would need to reveal their coupling before that bash. Yet a wave of procrastination prevented any action.

So, their relationship and Warren's new identity remained a secret. An unfamiliar twist on being in the closet. Despite their new roles, their past history of living together made for an elegantly easy transition with only a few speed bumps.

For Warren, making love to Paul was a stretch. He worried about falling into a trap of imagining he was with Rebecca and would close his eyes during sex. He was shredded between not wanting Paul to be a substitute for Rebecca and still wanting to feel her essence. Thankfully, two months into their sexual engagement brought his struggle to acceptance so he could be present and open with Paul. Warren continued to be surprised about the sexual experience with Paul. He had acclimated to the male body with the ease of a piano prodigy. As though he instinctively knew which keys or body parts to touch. Different yet the same with Rebecca. Warren remembered how he learned to pleasure Rebecca; she had been a patient teacher. But with Paul, it came naturally. He was unsure what they meant but the orgasms he achieved with Rebecca were on the same level as with Paul. Warren wanted to stop overthinking his sexuality because it was nonproductive.

So far, Paul had remained faithful to Warren, but he worried that it was a façade. He bravely told Warren, "You know how I've never settled down with anyone. In fact, you are the first person I could say *I love you* to. I've never believed in fidelity. Things are different with you. Right now, I can't imagine having sex with anyone else, but I can't commit to it forever. It isn't fair to you. I don't want to hurt you, and I don't want to lie. I hope you understand."

"I know what your history with men has been. Rebecca was pretty open about you. And I get what you are saying. I don't like it. If I can be monogamous, I don't quite understand why you wouldn't be able to. But look, I love you. I want to be with you. If that's your one flaw, I guess I can live with it."

Warren had to get accustomed to his new bisexual identity if he had to label himself. He'd heard of the prejudice against bisexuals. There was skepticism that bisexuals were really gay and were hiding behind their bisexual identity. But for Warren that wasn't true. He wasn't hiding any gayness. When he Googled bisexuality, he found that closeted bisexual men want to continue having sexual and emotional relationships with both men and women but they feared stigmatization and being ostracized from their communities. That confused Warren further. He wasn't part of any community. He only wanted to have a permanent relationship with Paul.

On their three-month anniversary, Warren and Paul branched out of their cocoon. Two celebrations were called for. Warren had reached a milestone with his fingernails. The chewing had stopped and his hands had returned to their original condition. They crossed off their favorite local haunt, Il Forno, where Warren and Rebecca had been ensconced as honorary patrons. Getting out of Santa Monica proper was the solution. They picked Ruth Chris Steakhouse in Beverly Hills, an old-guard festive restaurant where they could be incognito.

After parking, they strolled Beverly Drive before their eight-p.m. seating. When Paul clasped Warren's hand, paranoia caused Warren to bristle.

"What if someone sees us?"

Paul tried to calm Warren with, "Don't worry. No one is going to care. It's Beverly Hills; we don't know anyone here."

"I work just up the street."

"Okay, but you're going to make up for this when we get home."

A playfulness shot into gear; they turned into a dark alley and Warren quickly kissed Paul.

At Ruth Chris Steakhouse, Warren requested a booth in their main room. The air of romanticism filled the room with the smell of peppercorn sauce on steak whisked for them when they were seated.

During dinner, they acted like children touching their legs hidden behind the white tablecloths. Arthur J, their waiter, asked with a subtle wink, "Can I suggest the Porterhouse for Two?"

Warren said, "I swear he knows we're lovers."

Paul said, "He's just trying to let us get comfortable. I'm sure he's gay. I'll have to teach you gaydar."

Warren laughed and told Paul, "I love porterhouse steaks. Did you know they go back to the Industrial Revolution? In London, a "Porter House" was a chophouse known for serving steaks and ales, including London's new porter-style beers popular in the 1750s.

Paul giggled, "You're just full of trivia. But you're wrong, in 1814 on Manhattan's Pearl Street, large T-bone steaks were named Porter House."

"How appropriate that we live on Pearl Street."

The gourmet intensity of each course built to a wicked chocolate soufflé finale. While they were savoring the soufflé, Paul kissed Warren on the cheek and whispered, "Happy anniversary, my love."

Warren beamed back, "I love you." On the drive back to Ocean Garden, Paul tentatively said, "Now that we've come out, what do you think about socializing? A dinner with Teresa and Jackie."

Warren countered, "Without any warning about what's going on with us?"

"There isn't anything to tell. They'll get subtle hints. When they see how happy we are, they aren't going to care."

"I think you're living in a fantasy world, Paul. This is big. Brothers-in-law falling in love plus me changing my sexuality."

"It's 2017, not the Middle Ages. Have some faith in them."

Warren reluctantly complied. The inviting part was easy. They were both free on the first Saturday of the new year. Warren tried to avoid being unhinged during the week. Paul handled the menu and spotless cleaning so Warren could focus on a new eviction case. The tenant from hell refused to leave her Culver City abode. She'd committed the sin of deducting what she called emergency repairs from her monthly rent and breaking the rule of no dogs over twenty-five pounds.

On Saturday afternoon a call from Teresa pulsed on Warren's iPhone, "Warren, I'm sorry I have to cancel. I've come down with the flu. I don't want to infect you. I should have left work early yesterday." Warren's initial reaction was to call Jackie and cancel…a premonition that sitting at the dining room table with Jackie and Paul, Jackie might explode. Paul convinced Warren that it would be a non-event if Jackie discovered their relationship.

Seeing Jackie's face for the first time since Rebecca's death that evening brought Warren a wistful melancholy of Rebecca. Warren had been warding off any contact with Jackie using the excuse of work. He'd wanted to avoid his incomprehensible relationship with Paul until this dinner.

The dinner conversation went from banal to diary reporting, up until the dessert of lemon tarts arrived.

"So, what's really going on with you guys? You both seem so happy. Of course, I was worried about both of you after Rebecca died. You were both so close to her. It was almost like you were in a threesome."

Paul took Warren's hand and replied, "We're actually doing okay." Warren's quotient of happiness nervously rose to the surface while Paul spoke.

"What is this? Why are you guys holding hands?"

Warren froze and pulled his hand away. His initial reaction was to bail.

Paul said, "We've gotten very close, Jackie. I think Rebecca would approve."

The rage in Jackie's eyes was strong enough to sear through Paul and Warren.

"Are you kidding? Rebecca would be horrified, just like me. This is like incest. It's a sick joke."

Warren spoke, "We're not blood relatives. We're brothers-in-law. Don't throw the term *incest* around."

Paul completed, "We're adults. I know you're shocked, but Rebecca would have wanted us to be happy. We were surprised that this happened."

"How the fuck could you do this, Paul? You were so close. Rebecca took care of you; let you live here. Put up with your bullshit. This is a great payback."

Paul cried, "You don't know everything about us. We took care of each other. I was always there for my sister."

Jackie was a lion prowling the dining room with her killer declarations.

"Warren, how could you dishonor your wife and your marriage? What kind of crap is this? You were gay through the whole marriage and now that Rebecca is gone, you're coming out? What kind of fuckin' soap opera are you playing out?"

Warren responded, "Please, Jackie, don't label me. I'm not gay. You know how much I loved Rebecca. I would never hurt her."

"Warren, I was friends with Rebecca for twenty years. You don't realize the sacrifices she made in the marriage. Your long working hours when you were absent. You probably caused her miscarriage."

Warren and Paul had been scorched by Jackie's ranting. Warren's stomach wanted to detonate from Jackie's accusations. She continued, "You expect me to believe anything you say? Were you sleeping with other men? Is this an image thing? You wanted everyone to think you were straight?"

"Oh God no, I am straight, or I mean maybe bisexual. I can't help it if I fell in love with Paul."

"No, you couldn't. You're a fucking jerk. I'm leaving. You can go on fucking each other for all I care."

When Jackie left, Paul approached Warren asking for forgiveness for allowing the evening to occur. Warren folded his arms together blockading Paul.

"I knew this would happen, Paul. What have we done? Jackie thinks it's sick and that we are a disgrace to Rebecca."

"You know it isn't. We love each other. We're not hurting anybody. Jackie is just shocked. She doesn't understand. And it's just Jackie. I'm sure when Teresa and Melody find out that they won't care."

Warren said, "I hope you're right. For now, I don't want any more drama."

Paul's vision of acceptance of their unique relationship came true. Melody, Teresa, and his clients all came to their defense. The diverse multi-generational Ocean Garden never questioned the relationship. For Paul's circle, it was never an issue. Uncle Buddy had been told but his dementia had slammed his brain processing. The only outlier was Larry, the attorney whose office was adjacent to Warren's. During the months before Rebecca died and after, he'd pitched in with cases in limbo, emergency court appearances, and other deadlines that Teresa couldn't assist with.

When the rumor factory at the office hit about Warren's relationship with Paul, Warren had an inkling that conservative and religious Larry might have issues.

On their walk to their weekly lunch at Factor's, Larry tentatively said, "I know we're basically working acquaintances, but since Rebecca passed, I thought we'd become friends. So, I heard the craziest office gossip, that you're involved with your brother-in-law."

"Yes. I can't explain exactly what happened, but yes, we're in a relationship."

"Does that mean you're gay, Warren?"

"No, not necessarily. I think I'm bisexual. I don't like labels. This is private anyway."

"Don't give me that bullshit about people should love who they want to. I know you're not religious. I hate to get into a religious discussion."

"Then don't. Let's talk about something else. This doesn't affect you."

"You know it's a sin in the bible, in Leviticus."

"Look, Larry, you can believe what you want, but don't be judgmental."

"And what about the fact that Paul is your brother-in-law? That's a sin, too."

"You know, Larry, I appreciate how you've helped at work, but I'm not going to stand for you talking to me like this. You are humiliating yourself. I've lost my appetite, and I'm going to skip lunch. I'm walking back to the office."

Warren's chest felt unshackled on his return to work.

Later that fall, Warren told Paul, "You know I've been thinking about something. I know I said we can live in our little bubble. That it would be enough. But I got to thinking. What about a child? Someone with our DNA. A legacy we could leave. All our best qualities, taught to a new generation. The child I wanted to have with Rebecca. What do you think?"

Paul was flabbergasted. He couldn't believe Warren was telling him this plan. A child. A little Rebecca girl or a boy. Paul never thought about being a parent. He never thought he'd fall in love and live with someone. Parenting was a big deal. It would have a profound effect on their relationship having a third person in their lives.

"Are you thinking clearly, Warren? Not only is it a big responsibility but think about how everything would change. You see how new parents act. Everything is focused on the child. And we'd be so tired. I bet we'd stop having sex." Before he could finish, Warren was ravishing him and dragging Paul upstairs.

In the morning, Paul told Warren, "I've been thinking about what you said. I realize this would be a chance for me to finally grow up. Not thinking about myself. I'd have a purpose."

"But listen, Paul, it needs to be an unselfish reason. Something both of us really want."

Paul finalized the conversation with, "I keep thinking Rebecca would have wanted this."

<h1 style="text-align:center">Chapter 25</h1>
Baby

2018 brought riches to both Warren and Paul. Warren's practice expanded. Teresa passed the bar, and she became more of a <u>rainmaker</u> than Warren because of her 5,000 millennial friends on Facebook that needed attorney services. Melody became an invaluable legal secretary and office manager. Paul was teaching three classes at Santa Monica College and was on track for a full-time position.

But the most significant New Year's event was the baby quest. Their fantasy was to have a child with both of their DNA. At the Santa Monica In Vitro clinic, they gave Paul and Warren literature that explained combining two sperm was impossible because there aren't enough goodies in the sperm to sustain an embryo. The result of reading further confused them with talk about fertilizing multiple eggs if the DNA were removed that could cause twins.

When they met with Dr. Klein he came up with a possible solution.

"So, Warren, if you had a close relative, we could transfer her eggs into the surrogate and use Paul's sperm to fertilize the eggs. That way the child would be biologically connected to both of you."

Warren was an only child so that part eliminated the close relative scenario from the equation.

"Doctor Klien, when you say close relative would that also include a cousin?"

"Possibly. The DNA would be further removed, so the intended results might not be worth the additional expense of the procedure."

After they tried to digest the medical jargon, Warren told Paul, "I think we should just use your sperm. I want Rebecca's legacy to continue. I don't care about myself. With your sperm, we'd be creating a piece of Rebecca…a biological connection."

Paul acquiesced, wanting to not only make Warren happy but excited about giving Rebecca a child. With their lives in a bubble, having a child would expand their universe.

Once they found a surrogate, Warren's lawyering skills and contacts would ensure that all the legal papers would be worked out relating to the surrogate. The complicated process included ensuring the health of the surrogate, along with testing for genetic diseases or disorders.

Julie was the third surrogate they met with. She had just graduated from USC and was saddled with over $100,000 in student loans; so surrogacy would provide her a path to reducing the burden. Her smile brightened the room similar to the stir that Rebecca created when she made an entrance, but there were differences. She used makeup, had more of a boxy figure, and stood taller. Yet she had an essence that reminded them of Rebecca. Her plucky spirit won them over. Premium Surrogacy vetted her and checked off all the boxes. None of the family history was alarming. Her father had type two diabetes, her fraternal grandmother had breast cancer, and paternal grandfather had old age dementia. The family was blessed with longevity. Julie still lived at home with her parents because of her debt and planned to remain there during the pregnancy. She'd broached the plan with her parents but until she actually became pregnant, she didn't want to alarm them.

When Paul and Warren had their debriefing, Warren's frown declared, "I'm worried that her parents might not be on board."

Paul said, "Let's not worry about that. As a plan B, she could live with us. Don't you love her spunk? And having a boxy figure will make for an easy birth."

Warren said, "How would you know that?"

"I've been binge-watching *The Midwife* on PBS. I could be the midwife for Julie!"

On March 31, 2018, Paul and Warren were trying to decide how to honor the one-year anniversary since Rebecca had died.

"Do you think it's too cold to go to the beach? Rebecca loved the beach. That's where she was the happiest."

Paul concurred and said, "I can't believe what's happened in the last year. It's our six-month anniversary and we're looking at becoming fathers!" The brisk morning developed into a chilly but blistering sunny afternoon. Perfect for cuddling. They grabbed their leather jackets, scarves and wool caps. Paul said, "It looks like we're dressed for a blizzard."

When they went to their garage, the iPhone began vibrating, showing Julie's name.

"Hi. Is everything okay?" Each time Julie called, the pit in their stomachs kept getting larger. Was she changing her mind? Did she want more money?

"I think I might be pregnant. I have to get an appointment at the clinic to take the test. My period is three weeks late, and I didn't want to tell you guys. You know, get your hopes up and then be let down. I've never been this late before."

"Should we go with you tomorrow?"

"Would you guys? It's kinda scary for me, and I would love for you to be there. I mean it's going to be your child."

"Just let us know when you get your appointment, and we'll make sure we can be there." There was an eruption of tears when they embraced.

Warren said, "It's a sign from Rebecca, like she's sending us a present. Letting us know that she approves of what we're doing. I hope it's a girl so we can name her Becky." For Paul, the day at the beach memorializing Rebecca turned into a planning session about renovating his old bedroom to become "baby ready." But Warren was petrified of unlocking the same steps he and Rebecca had taken six years ago, worried that it would jinx Julie's pregnancy. He decided to wipe out those memories and start fresh; he would let Paul make the decision about baby furniture and room color. Warren's goal was to make Julie happy and healthy to ensure a safe and successful birth of their child.

At the appointment on Tuesday, the doctor confirmed Julie's pregnancy status and told her, "Congratulations, it looks like you'll be giving birth in December."

Paul asked, "What about the Lamaze classes? Are they necessary?" Paul had recurring nightmares of the horror show experience with Rebecca and her miscarriage.

"I think it's a good idea. You could try something online but the camaraderie between other future mothers is important. You have time to decide. I don't suggest you attend classes until the end of the second trimester."

The first ultrasound was taken eight weeks into the pregnancy, reflecting the gestational sac and fetal heartbeat. Julie bragged about her first trimester not hitting her with nausea or vomiting. A blown-up copy of the ultrasound was plastered to the townhouse refrigerator along with the screensaver on their respective laptops and home screens on their iPhones. They never missed an opportunity to brag to friends and strangers.

Chapter 26
Baby Two

Paul's night classes were igniting with Advanced Audition Workshop, Stage Movement for Actors and Beginning Stage Direction. The cross-generational students kept him engaged. Despite the draining energy of being on his feet teaching for two hours, he had not felt this fulfilled in an eternity. The short walk back to Ocean Garden at nine after his session was rejuvenating.

"Hey, Mr. Burke? Can I talk to you about class?"

Startled, Paul turned around and faced Greg, a young actor in his Audition Workshop. Greg's honey hair, ocean blues, six feet height and unobtrusive nose were generic and didn't surprise Paul that he'd gotten no traction in the audition process.

"If you don't mind walking this direction while we talk. I live on Pearl and 28th."

Greg said, "Can I drive you? My car is in the lot. It won't take much time."

Paul was bushed, so agreed to let Greg take him back to Ocean Garden.

"I'm so frustrated with auditioning. I hate the rejections. And these guys I'm competing with are not only gorgeous, but they are super confident."

"You need to forget what you've been doing during auditions in the past and start from scratch."

"Yeh, yeh. You keep telling us that."

Before they reached Greg's car, he invaded Paul's space and started kissing him. Paul tried to push him away but Greg's height dug into him.

"Stop it, Greg. I'm in a relationship."

"I saw you flirting with me. Come on. I think you are so hot."

Paul felt an erection brewing and threw himself into a kaleidoscope of choices. He'd missed the buzz of one-night stands and the feel of a new untested body. *You're going to be a father. Why would I jeopardize my relationship with Warren? But I want this guy. It's been almost a year. Fuck.*

Greg kept pawing at him like he was a piece of meat. Finally, he escaped from Greg's clutches.

"Greg, this is inappropriate. I'm tempted to report this incident to the department chair. I don't want to do that. We can just pretend this didn't happen. It's up to you whether you want to remain in my class."

Greg said, "That's fine. I'll just drop the class. You're not much of a teacher anyway."

Paul jogged back to Ocean Garden disgusted that Greg had not apologized and felt guilty about what almost happened. He didn't know if he should tell Warren since he had not committed an infraction. He had discovered the byproduct of being in love was questioning the consequences of his action. Paul wanted these scary real emotions to stop. When Paul arrived at Ocean Garden, Warren's grin made him float. He played a voicemail from Julie, "Guys, we should party. I think I sense a heartbeat and I want you to feel it."

After screaming until they became hoarse, it was decided that the celebration should occur at Il Forno, and when they texted Julie, she concurred. Enough time had passed that the duo of

Warren and Paul was no longer a secret along with their impending parenthood. When Julie arrived at Ocean Garden the following evening, Paul was first given the honor of listening for the heartbeat since it was his sperm that was responsible for this miracle. Julie sat on the dining room chair, while Paul bent down and pressed his ear against her stomach. Warren hovered over him wanting to feel the vibration emanating from Julie to Paul to him. The faint heartbeat built to a crescendo. Paul's face exploded but when Warren changed places with Paul, he looked confused because he couldn't hear anything.

Julie said, "Just wait, the baby may be sleeping."

Warren shrieked, "It's kicking!"

Julie's miraculous smile filled the room and she said, "You guys really are something. You are going to make the best parents."

The Il Forno staff knew about Paul and Warren's coupling along with their baby-making plan but this was the first time they'd met Julie.

'Who is this lovely lady?"

Warren said, "She's having our baby. We are here to celebrate because we heard the heartbeat for the first time and even some mean kicking!" The patrons heard the declaration and applause erupted. Julie was a trooper and didn't drink any alcohol during the feast, but she was rewarded a surprise entree by the chef. He prepared a specially designed delicacy. The linguine with lobster, scallops, shiitake mushrooms, fresh tomatoes and creamy red bell pepper sauce took Julie into ecstasy.

They refused to let the enchanted evening end so the owner had to evict them from the restaurant at the ten p.m. closing time.

When they walked Julie to her car and said goodbye, Paul said, "Can I just listen to the heartbeat one more time? I want to make sure I wasn't imagining the sound."

After Warren and Julie stopped giggling, he said, "Come on, let Julie go. She needs her sleep so she can keep up her strength."

Before Julie left, Warren handed her a large bag, "Don't forget this care package. I had the chef put together enough food to feed an army, now that you are eating for two."

Back at the townhouse, Paul said, "Are we really going to make great parents like Julie said? What do we know about bringing up a girl?"

Warren said, "Are you kidding? Look at your relationship with Rebecca. Sometimes I think you knew more about her than I did. Isn't that the cliché, that gay men understand women better than a straight guy. I loved your sister, but I didn't always get what was going on in her head."

"But there are so many things about being a parent. What's going to happen when she gets her period?"

"That's in 13 years!!"

"But she is going to need some women in her life."

"Don't worry. Melody and Teresa are like family. We'll be fine."

Paul was afraid to tell Warren about the elephant in the room, that he had almost strayed. What kind of example would that be for a child? Would Warren be forgiving if he found out? Paul tried convincing himself that once he became a father, he would be transformed into a monogamous partner unable to transgress. Rebecca needed to be proud of Paul.

Chapter 27
Baby Three

At the end of July, twenty weeks into the pregnancy, the second ultrasound was scheduled. The night before the event, Warren and Paul couldn't sleep.

Warren queried, "Do we really want to know the sex of our baby now or let it be a surprise?"

"Yes, so we can figure out the finishing touches in the nursery and finalize names."

Julie met Warren and Paul at the clinic. While the sonographer, Francine, performed the ultrasound, she explained each step of the test and what they were looking for in the four chambers of the heart and important organs like the kidneys.

Warren and Paul asked in unison, "What about the sex?"

The sonographer told them, "Congrats, you are going to have a healthy girl."

Paul and Warren were jumping out of their skin from the news that a little baby girl that they would name Becky was growing inside of Julie.

Warren's attorney mind wanted proof and he asked, "How can we tell looking at the ultrasound that it's a girl?"

She pointed to the monitor and said, "If the placenta is forming on the left side of the uterus, it will most likely be a girl."

During the exhilaration, they were ignoring the sniveling from Julie. Warren and Paul went into panic mode, suspecting Julie was changing her mind. Before they could ask her, she said, "This is so emotional. It didn't quite seem so real even when we felt the kicking. It was so difficult to make out the image on the first ultrasound. This time around it's clear that there is life."

"You're sure you're okay, Julie?"

"Yes, don't worry, I'm not changing my mind. This is going to be your child. And I am so happy that I can give you that." That triggered a splash of tears from Paul and Warren.

On a weekly basis, Warren or Paul would visit Julie. Paul sat near Julie and read to her stomach the musical words of *Jazz Baby* by Lisa Wheeler. He would snap his fingers and sing the words. He wanted the growing infant to get used to his voice and smell. He brought along a stuffed chimpanzee and rubbed it on Julie's stomach. After birth, he hoped that the baby would be comforted by the smell.

Julie's due date was the first week in December. Paul was gung-ho about completing the fully stocked nursery. He asked his set decorator from *P.S. Your Cat is Dead* to paint butterflies on the yellow wall of the bedroom.

At the point where Lamaze training would be appropriate, Warren told Paul, "I looked at the schedule, and I don't think I'll be able to take Julie each week."

It was as though a snake had bitten Paul with a venom that brought back the memory of his Lamaze experience with Rebecca.

Paul tried to respond with *Warren, but I can't do it.* Instead, he shuddered. Warren realized his mistake and he pacified Paul with a hug.

"Oh, God, I'm sorry. Of course, I wouldn't expect you to go with Julie." Thankfully, Paul nor Rebecca never traumatized

Warren with a detailed description of what went on that day. But Warren's gut knew it was devastating.

Paul countered with, "You know I should be able to teach Julie the methods I learned," so he added the exercises to his daily visits to Julie.

The fourth trimester and Thanksgiving snuck up on them. Uncle Buddy, in remission from his dementia; his partner, Harry; Teresa, Melody, Paul's ex, Joshua; Alexander and Garth assembled for the feast. During the demolition of the Heritage Turkey, each guest volunteered a unanimous chorus of thanks for the upcoming birth of Becky. After dinner, Paul and Warren were treated to a surprise baby shower. A gasp came when they opened the pacifier clip, baby booties, bath support, and a versatile diaper backpack.

The only missing element was the no-show of Jackie. Despite her tirade last year, Warren and Paul reached out for a reconciliation, but their calls remained unanswered.

The conversation floated to what life would be like with an infant. Teresa did most of the drilling, "So guys, have you figured out who will do what? You do realize what it's like raising an infant."

Paul jumped in with, "Yes, we've got it covered. Our work schedules are perfect. I work evenings when Warren will be here. And if I have an audition, Warren's office is conveniently close by for emergencies." Behind the scenes, both Paul and Warren were as apprehensive as pets dreading firecrackers on the Fourth of July.

The stars became aligned and on Sunday, December ninth they received a call from Julie, "It's time. My water just broke." They drove to nearby Culver City, where Julie had been living with her parents. Her parents' initial reaction to Julie being a surrogate was abhorrence. As they got used to the idea and when they met Warren and Paul, they slowly became supportive. The literature said that if the surrogate mother can remain in her home, it would offer the best outcome. The paperwork involving Warren and Paul being legal parents to the newborn had already been signed, sealed and delivered. The last step was for Julie to give birth. By the time she was admitted to WHS she was dilating and the contractions were less than five minutes apart.

Warren and Paul had insisted they be part of the birthing process and able to be with Julie in the delivery room. Becky was an easy birth. The nurses and doctors said Julie had an efficient uterus that contracted with majestic strength, and a compliant birth canal. Watching Becky's grand entrance from Julie's womb became Warren and Paul's eighth wonder of the world. The cry heard round the delivery room from their purple baby was emboldening. The doctor asked if Paul and Warren wanted to cut the umbilical cord and they said, "Only if we can do it together." Warren stood behind Paul and held his nervous arms as they separated Becky from Julie's placenta with special scissors after the cord had been clamped. Purple Becky gradually turned to a light shade of pink. First Becky was placed on Julie's chest to confirm her sense of experiencing life outside of the womb. Then Warren and Paul were encouraged to play with the baby's feet and hands. This would be the beginning of the physical and emotional transfer of Becky from Julie to them. A good portion of Paul's DNA was visible with those similar ears along with piercing eyes like his sister's.

Warren and Paul were in awe of the bond between mother and child. A flashflood of tears streamed from the threesome's eyes. A respite before the intended parents and Julie prepared for the emotional transfer of Becky. The love between the four of them had been stretched to the rafters.

After Julie's discharge, Paul and Warren took her back to Culver City. Their agreement was for Julie to visit one final time two weeks after the delivery to give comfort to Becky and closure for Julie that the infant was adjusting to her new parents.

They were blessed with a happy infant who didn't incessantly cry. Becky slept a good portion of the evening on the initial night at Ocean Garden. Paul and Warren took turns when they heard her cry for milk at three a.m. The pre-planning along with the familiarity to their smell and voices helped with Becky's transition.

A week after the birth of Becky, Paul and Warren were snuggling on their bed, watching Netflix and Paul said, "You know, I want you to adopt Becky. She really is our child." Paul noticed that Warren was still wearing his wedding ring. Rebecca's death two years ago felt like yesterday and an eternity because of what had transpired. An out-of-the-box thought came to Paul, and he whispered, "Do you ever think about us getting married?" Warren did not respond, and when Paul heard a snoring sound, he realized that Warren had fallen asleep. Warren was on a treadmill trying to catch some shuteye.

At first, Warren thought the energy force and faint odor had aroused him until he realized it was the smell of coffee. He thought, *thank you my love for remembering to set the Keurig so we'd have fresh caffeine in the morning.* Rebecca looked consumed with finishing eight hours of sleep. The Land End's Supima sheets wrapped around her frame, a blonde beauty queen resting. Last night's love-making had guaranteed an unencumbered sleep for both of them. After Warren edged out from Rebecca's spooning embrace, Rebecca curled into the fetal position. Warren's scratchy eyes searched for the bathroom to relieve himself. The itch on his shaft was disconcerting. He hoped that the herpes outbreak had begun healing. Luckily, he'd filled the prescription for acyclovir quickly. The bathroom's marble tile cooled his feet and stretching his biceps energized Warren. He used his favorite oatmeal-colored washcloth to give himself a whore's bath, a quick sponge bath by hand. His stumpy fingertips needed rebandaging. He'd given up trying to break that habit of nail biting. He grabbed his cargo shorts and walked down the staircase to the main floor that housed the living and dining room along with the kitchen. He passed the rarely used front entrance at the end of the stairs because the kitchen had a door to the two-car garage in the back of the townhouse.

Since Rebecca had announced they were going to be parents last week, they'd been feasting on the thrill of having a child. Their shared DNA would create a testament to their values and love. With Rebecca's teaching position blocks away and Warren's office within five miles, their Ocean Garden townhouse was a jackpot winner of places to live. The cliché *it takes a village* took on a luscious meaning for them.

Sunday morning was Warren's favorite day. He would make gluten-free waffles smothered with Costco real maple syrup and blueberries. There was freshly ground Peet's coffee and pulpy Valencia orange juice. In the background, KUSC played the Mostly Mozart Program, while they would read the Los Angeles Times.

Warren walked back to the second floor to awaken his wife, but she wasn't in bed. Warren listened for the shower in the second bedroom but it was silent. Outside the bathroom, he saw the remains of a pouch sitting open on the bathroom counter. An oddity since she was so careful to keep it germ-free.

"Rebecca, where are you?" He checked the walk-in closet hoping she was deciding what sumptuous outfit she would be wearing, but it was empty. Rebecca may have been surveying the grounds looking for ripening lemons, figs, oranges, limes or flowers. The birds of paradise were in abundance and would make a lovely centerpiece for the round teak dining room table.

Warren began checking out the sports section in the paper until Rebecca returned. Underneath the newspaper, Warren found a letter. The official-looking court return address intrigued Warren to read further. Ah yes, it was about a partnership Rebecca had invested in with her brother. The letter looked ominous. This was ancient history. He wondered if the letter upset Rebecca. He continued reading that there was going to be a distribution of the funds. Warren hadn't remembered how much money was tied up in the company, Realtor Plus. He was relieved that most of the inheritance from Rebecca's mom had supplied them with a healthy deposit on their townhouse.

After half an hour Warren decided to scan the complex for Rebecca's location. The seventy-five townhouses imitated Palm Springs because the semi-private road circling the perimeter of the community ensured no street noises. The road was used for guest parking while the common areas were within the circle. Ocean Garden was blessed by not being a gated community which pleased Rebecca and Warren's sensibilities. A gated community would have given them a false sense of security and jailed isolation.

The eerie quiet for a Sunday morning disturbed Warren. Even the pool was empty. Normally, Alexandra and Garth would perch themselves on the pool lounges and be engulfed in the New York Times by now. The tennis court was vacant.

Rebecca's disappearance was out of character. Warren grabbed his I-phone and tried calling her number. After eight rings it went to voicemail. Odd. Rebecca was always good about answering and leaving the ringer on. Jaunting back to the townhouse and hoping Rebecca had returned lightened Warren's mood. The radio was off and there was a man sitting at the dining room table.

"Oh, hi, Warren. I wondered what happened to you. I'm starving. Becky finally slept through the night. Thank goodness, her teething has stopped. I was hoping we could make love this morning."

"Who are you? Get out of here or I'm calling the police."

"What? It's Paul. Stop fooling around. You're getting me scared."

Warren imagined this was a hallucination. Not only was Rebecca missing but a strange man who pretended to be his lover was in the dining room who knew Warren's name. And how could there be a baby upstairs sleeping?

Warren said, "Where's Rebecca?"

Warren's eyes began opening as his body was being shaken. Warren tumbled to the floor until Paul broke his fall. When he let out a roar of tears, he pushed Paul away.

While Warren's eyes were darting at the ceiling, the walls, and the floor, he rambled, "What have we done? This should be Rebecca's child. What's wrong with me? Trying to move on. I'm still married to her. She's still alive. I rehashed our life together. I recognized her smell when I was sleeping, and then I smelled the coffee percolating from the Keurig always set before we went to sleep."

It took mammoth strength for Paul to avoid collapsing with Warren. Warren's words scared him; something was out of kilter. Was the relationship and having a child a mistake? Quickly, Rebecca's admonition of *take care of Warren, he'll be lost without me* filled his head.

Warren slumped and said, "I didn't even recognize you. I was in an alternate universe. I'm losing it, Paul."

"No, you're just mourning the loss of Rebecca. You can't predict when it's going to happen. I know things have happened so fast."

The high drama was interrupted by Becky's hunger cries.

Warren jumped and gave Becky her formula. Paul held him from behind and said, "Do you know how much I love you, Warren?"

After Warren said, "Stop, you are going to make me cry again. I love you. You know maybe we should think about marriage? Don't freak out. I know how you used to feel about commitment. I want to adopt Becky. She has two fathers," all Paul could do was smile.

Once Becky was fed, Paul prepared breakfast while Warren primed himself for work. When Warren sat at the kitchen table and read the newspaper, Paul was relieved to see Warren's fingernails intact. But what made Paul smile was when he saw a discoloration above the knuckle on Warren's left hand; the fourth finger.

Despite the extra responsibility of caring for Becky, Paul and Warren felt like they were on a continuous honeymoon. Ocean Garden welcomed Becky with generous doses of their shared social ties and common perspectives. The unconditional assistance they offered humbled Warren and Paul. Babysitting offers, fat brain education toys, and the book, *Goodnight Stories for Rebel Girls*, filled their coffers…never judging this new addition to their family, fathered by two men who were brothers-in-law.

Paul had the brunt of responsibilities having to not only take care of Becky during the day but keeping the house in working order and food shopping. He joked with his friends that he felt like a 50s housewife or Stepford wife being supported by a husband or calling Warren a sugar daddy. He had decided to skip the winter semester teaching to focus on Becky and learning to be a mother and father. Becky acclimated to her surroundings outside of Julie's womb. Paul could spend hours staring at her while she soaked in sights and smells. When Julie visited two weeks later, she said, "I can't believe how much Becky has changed. I could swear she's aware of me."

"It's your smell and the sound of your voice. She may be cognizant of when she was in your womb. Pretty amazing, isn't it?"

"I was kinda' worried about this arrangement. That she'd be crying all the time and feel abandoned by her mother. But I can see I was wrong. You've really come through for her. I know she's in good hands."

"Warren said to say hello. He's involved with a big case that is going to trial so I've been taking up the slack with Becky. I don't mind."

When she left, Paul's iPhone buzzed.

"Paul, how did it go with Julie?"

"Excellent. She felt that Becky was in good hands. Kinda' scary that she'll be out of the picture."

"Yes, I know. Look, the trial is heating up and I might be doing an all-nighter. I don't want to, but I have to review my notes and the depositions before the trial next week."

"What would have happened if I had a class to teach tonight?"

"I've been thinking about that. I talked to Melody, and she said she'd pitch in for emergencies."

"Okay, I'll see you in the morning."

"Love you."

Paul tried not to project that Warren's action would be a recurring pattern. Becky's hunger cry flipped the switch of Paul's thoughts as he got the Enfamil Enspire formula ready to give comfort to Becky.

At four a.m. Warren's body insisted that he return to Ocean Garden. During his drive, he had to slap himself when his eyes began drooping. He ripped off his clothing and collapsed into bed with Paul. His remorse at not spending enough time with Paul and Becky was mounting.

Two hours had elapsed before Becky clamored for another formula. Amazingly, Warren's exhaustion allowed him to sleep despite Becky's cries. Paul had acquired a third sense of knowing

Becky's needs. He gently kissed Warren before his eyes popped open…like the pistol at the beginning of a race, and his daily drill began. The trip up and down the stairs gave him an aerobic workout gathering Becky's formula.

And his big baby, Warren, required a lunch of Turkish marinated skinless, boneless chicken breasts along with a salad with sixteen ingredients. Paul enjoyed cooking and loved Warren's praises and thanks, "You don't realize how much these gourmet delicious lunches mean to me. I hate going out for lunch. And in the morning, I'm usually so beat I don't want to worry about preparing anything. I love you."

Paul kept Becky engaged with Beethoven's Ninth and he read to her, *Ten Little Fingers* by Mem Fox. His day raced against the clock with keeping the townhouse top-notch clean that you could eat off the floor. On the nights that Warren made his entrance at a reasonable time when they could eat together, Paul was zonked.

Warren's recent case had resulted in a malpractice trial from a referral from Teresa. A friend of her nephew, Luis, had injured his hip playing basketball at school. After limping for a week, Luis visited his doctor. The X-ray showed a sprain. Luis was given crutches to relieve pressure but he still walked with a limp. Ultimately, he'd been misdiagnosed. If an MRI had been taken earlier, surgery would have corrected the injury. Because of the gap in time, after the operation, Luis was left with a limp. The hospital group offered $100,000, but Warren told his clients that there would be a much larger settlement if they went to trial. Warren asked for $500,000 to include pain and suffering. In medical malpractice, the burden is on the patient to prove that the medical provider deviated from the standard of care and caused harm. Warren believed he had proven that the bad surgical outcome was caused by negligence.

When the judge ruled against him, Warren cursed to himself. He'd explained to the clients how going to trial was the equivalent of Las Vegas gambling. Would they remember that? Would they try to sue Warren for malpractice because he had failed them? He had risked his clients being $100,000 richer rather than being kicked in the gut. He asked his clients, the Lees, to come to his office the next day for an explanation.

"I'm sorry things didn't go our way. The judge felt the hospital wasn't at fault."

Mr. Lee replied, "We understand. You did the best you could."

He had been greedy and now he would be on the hook for $20,000 of litigation expenses for expert witnesses and filing court costs. It was on contingency so Warren would slink away financially hollow. He began devouring his fingernails and fingertips.

Paul had planned a special dinner to celebrate the end of the trial. He told Warren that morning, "Good luck today. Now that the trial is over, I hope our life can get back to normal. You've hardly been spending any time with Becky. She'll think I'm her only parent. Please surprise me with dessert tonight."

Warren arrived at six, the earliest he had been home in months. Warren wanted to nap before facing Paul until he saw the painstaking preparations with freshly cut gardenias as a table centerpiece. Paul had lit candles from Boys Smell that jam-packed the townhouse with the smells of fig and sandalwood.

Paul greeted him with a rejuvenating kiss that temporarily let Warren forget the crushing events of his day. Warren kept his hands hidden, not wanting Paul to see the damage.

"Honey, you don't look very happy."

"No, we lost the trial."

"Oh, I'm sorry, Warren. What happens now?"

"I don't want to talk about it. Let's just eat."

The subdued dinner left the conversation to Paul detailing his news flash reporting on Becky. Without much response, Paul said, "You know it's really getting to me taking care of Becky. I was hoping we could hire a part time nanny."

Warren lashed out with, "Are you kidding? Do you realize how much money I'm out? I have two full-time employees and rent that I need to cover each month. Insurance companies have been cracking down. The days of steady settlements are long gone."

Paul's daggers came out when he retaliated, "Well at least you could share in the responsibility with Becky. It's like I'm raising her alone."

"Come on, Paul. This is just temporary. You're only working part-time. Anyway, I thought you liked doing this." The normally orgasmic food tasted rancid.

"It's been three months nonstop, working my ass off with the cleaning and the shopping. You wanted this child, Warren."

"No, this was a joint decision. We wanted Rebecca's legacy to continue."

Paul became unbridled and slammed out, "Really, Warren, I wonder if you just wanted my sperm so you could have a piece of Rebecca."

"You know that's not true. I love you."

"And having Becky solidifies our relationship? I don't want to feel trapped. And I did not give up teaching full time for you to treat me like this."

Becky broke the scourge with her cry for nourishment. Warren jumped and skittered up the stairs.

Paul told him, "She needs her formula. It's in the refrigerator. Remember, don't rush Becky. Touch the nipple to her lower lip and wait for her to open her mouth. Don't force the nipple into her mouth."

Warren turned around, took the formula and marched back upstairs. When she saw Warren, Becky screeched. He tried following Paul's directions but wanted her cries to cease with the formula. She gulped the formula quickly and within minutes started regurgitating all over Warren's shirt. He screamed for Paul's help.

"Oh, God. I told you not to let her drink so fast. Here, I'll take care of her. You need to get your shirt cleaned up." Warren crawled back from his lost battle.

Warren felt defeated as an attorney and a father before he went to bed. When Paul got into bed two hours later, he took on the shame they both felt with their vindictive words. At first, the makeup sex was robotic until it turned into tiger fighting and ultimately a born-again baptism of love.

The next morning Paul tried to repair the damage Warren had done to his swollen, red and tender nails. He put each finger into his mouth and was able to soothe the breaks in the skin that Warren's teeth had made. He followed up with antibacterial soap in warm water before he bandaged the digits.

The following weeks showed improvement with Warren exercising restraint on his workaholic hours. Each night he read to Becky until he fell asleep from his own exhaustion. He kept repeating, "Daddy loves you." By April, Becky was copying Warren's goofy facial expression. Warren shared in shopping duties by making a pit stop at Trader Joe's before returning each evening.

On the first Friday night of May he told Paul, "Hey, I've got good news. I've got a new case. It's a biggie. The client has a million-dollar policy. The housekeeper for one of those Santa Monica eyesore houses on 30th Street fell and she had a bunch of broken bones. She was hospitalized for a week."

Paul held his tongue from projecting negative thoughts of Warren falling back into long work hours.

"I see your face wondering if I'll be missing in action because of work. Don't worry. Teresa is going to take the lead on this. She'll do the depositions and find expert witness doctors."

"Warren, I got a notice from the college, and they were asking if I could teach evening classes this summer."

"Oh, definitely. Go ahead and say yes. I think we should let Melody babysit as a test. That way if I have to work on the night when you are teaching, she can pitch in for an emergency."

On the first day of June, while she was able to sit up in her Graco highchair, she banged on the tray with her hands and cried when Warren and Paul ate scrambled eggs filled with cheddar cheese, onions, and mushrooms. But once they fed Becky real food, and she got to use her hands, she giggled with joy.

A week before Paul's summer teaching position began, Becky changed. She stopped sleeping through the night and a mysterious rash formed around her mouth. When she started rubbing her ears, Warren and Paul thought it was a cute affectation until she began drooling. The doctor said it was teething and told them to rub their fingertips over her gums with gauze. Those same fingertips that Paul had healed when he sucked on them. Becky had been rubbing her ears to ease the ache of her teeth growing out of her gums.

Her outbursts were hammering nails into Paul's skull and Warren's work hours were becoming erratic. Each night his dinner appearance went from seven to eight to nine to ten.

"You promised me, Warren. You said Teresa would take the brunt of the work on your new big case."

"It's gotten too complicated for her."

"I'm starting class next week so you'd better make sure Melody is on call if you can't be here."

Warren's distracted eyes angered Paul. Warren was in sleep catchup mode after his horrendous pattern of chronic sleep deprivation that started during the trial from hell. Warren slept through Becky's every two-hour-teething episode.

When Paul decided to take her temperature, it showed 101. He panicked with thoughts of *Oh, God, she's sick. We've got to take her to the emergency room. I can't believe Warren is sleeping through her screeching. This is too much for me alone. This isn't working. I need a break. I don't want to be a wife or a parent. Warren wanted this and dumped the responsibility on me.*

Paul went back to the bedroom to awaken Warren.

"She's got a fever. What should we do?"

Warren groggily said, "Isn't there a twenty-four-hour urgent care nurse you can call?"

"Why don't you do that, Warren? I hardly had any sleep."

"You haven't been working fifteen-hour days like me. Don't be a brat, just call. I'm sure it's nothing." Warren shoved his pillow on his head and dove back into REM sleep.

Paul explained to the urgent care nurse by phone and she confirmed "It's probably teething. If the temperature doesn't go down, then bring her to urgent care."

When he rechecked Becky's temperature it had dropped to 98.6. A wave of relief and fury at Warren hit Paul as he crawled back to the master bedroom. When his head hit the pillow, Paul's sprinting thoughts prevented sleep. It felt like the strong shell around Paul, Becky and Warren had a hairline crack. In the morning, he would duel it out with Warren with new rules, or he would have to resort to plan "B."

"Warren, you are treating me like I'm an indentured wife. This doesn't feel like a partnership. Did you treat Rebecca this way?"

"You know I didn't. You don't get it. Do you realize how much money we're spending? And I'm the responsible one. It's my salary that is paying for everything; your car and health insurance and we've got three mouths to feed now. And these fancy baby supplies."

"Don't you want the best for Becky? She's our child. Maybe I should get a full-time job and then you'll see how much it will cost for daycare. You're getting a bargain with me."

"What do you want me to do?"

"I don't know. But you could start by making me feel that my taking care of Becky is just as important as your job. Not assuming that I'm always going to bail you out when it comes to Becky."

"I love you. Isn't that enough?" Paul wanted to say no, but instead, he walked away. He ignored Warren's, "Look, we'll talk tonight. I've got a meeting with the client and have to get ready for them." Warren grabbed the daily lunch Paul had prepared and sped off to his office. During the short commute, the chewing of his nails gave him a chance to avoid thinking he was a shit.

In the townhouse, Becky returned to her crying tirade, giving Paul a diversion from anger towards Warren. While he was giving Becky her formula, he felt an itch around his crotch. When he later noticed a reddish pimple on his shaft, he realized it was herpes. Another reason for directing rage at Warren. Now he had been infected by the virus, and it would never completely leave his system, thanks to Warren.

In the afternoon, Becky's coyote-like scream forced Paul to check for fever and saw that it had spiked to 102. He texted Warren at the office to meet him at the Culver City Pediatric Urgent Care. The Urgent Care office of wall-to-wall couples and shrieking children took Paul into a torture chamber. He tried texting and calling Warren again but got no response. Becky had fallen asleep and her head did not feel as warm so he asked the starched nurse, "How long of a wait is it going to be?"

"We're running behind. The earliest would be an hour but with this crowd it will probably be two hours."

A nearby mother said, "You have such a beautiful little girl. Don't you hate this place? I try to avoid coming here unless it's really an emergency. Where is her mother? It's so rare to see any fathers here."

Paul wasn't in the mood to explain Warren and Becky's origins. He had not enlisted to be in this emotional and physical inferno. Becky's smile and giggling had signaled her recovery.

"Come on, Becky, we're getting out of here."

During the drive back to Ocean Garden, Paul rehashed, *How could Warren ignore his cries for help? What is wrong with me for staying here?*

The steep descent of Warren's day crippled his morning workflow because his conversation with Paul before he left, plastered him with guilt. *What the fuck have I done? I'm straight. I've fallen in love with my dead wife's brother. We have used Paul's sperm to create a new Rebecca. And now I'm being a shitty parent and a fucked-up lover.*

Because of a productive afternoon, Warren had forgotten that his iPhone had been silenced all day. He shivered when he saw multiple texts and phone messages from Paul. Something was wrong with Becky and to meet him at Urgent Care. Because Paul wasn't answering his phone, Warren bulleted to Urgent Care, only to find there was no record of Paul or Becky.

When he arrived back at Ocean Garden, he checked upstairs and both Paul and Becky were in a cloud of sleep. Whatever calamity there was had been solved. Warren went to the kitchen and found leftovers which he gobbled without chewing... he had done enough chewing of his fingernails during the last twelve hours. Ready for sleep, he wiggled into bed and spooned with Paul. He longed for recovery when the sun rose in the morning. He would beg Paul to forgive him and convince Paul that he would change.

In the morning, the blinds kept the sunrise from waking Paul, and Warren edged out from Paul's spooning embrace. The itch on Warren's shaft was still disconcerting. He hoped that the herpes outbreak had begun healing. Luckily, he'd filled the prescription for acyclovir quickly. He knew he was infectious with the first sign of an outbreak and Paul would kill him if he got herpes.

Adding to his dilapidated morning, his damn stumpy fingertips needed rebandaging because he had given up trying to break that nasty habit. Looking for redemption, Warren decided to surprise Paul by preparing breakfast.

He whipped together steel cut oats, quinoa and freshly picked oranges from Ocean Garden. Upon completion, Warren walked back to the second floor to awaken him, but Paul wasn't in bed. Becky was sleeping in the nursery.

"Paul, where are you?" He checked the walk-in closet, but it was empty.

Warren decided to jog through the complex in search of Paul, feeling secure that abandoning Becky for fifteen minutes was safe.

Paul's disappearance was out of character. Warren grabbed his iPhone and tried calling his number. After eight rings it went to voicemail. Odd. Paul was always good about answering and leaving the ringer on. Jaunting back to the townhouse and hoping Paul had returned lightened Warren's mood.

On the usually naked living room coffee table, a folded paper appeared.

Dear Warren,

How could you not answer my text or call, about Becky? What is wrong with you? I'm sorry, but if I don't leave, I'm afraid I'll become monstrous with you. I know you try to be a good lover and father but I can't do this any longer. I didn't sign up for this. I don't want the responsibility. I've left you instructions on how to care for Becky. It's just too hard. Oh, thanks for giving me herpes.

Paul

Warren's squawked "Fuck" alerted the townhouse of impending doom. *No warning. Paul just walked away. No discussion. No second chance. A spoiled brat. How did I infect Paul? I thought I was so careful. Maybe I deserve this? Why didn't he call the general office number or Melody?* Warren proceeded to text Paul to be forgiven.

Paul, please come back. I know I fucked up. You probably don't believe me because I've asked you to forgive me before. I need you. Can we at least talk about this?

Then Warren went into overdrive about combining work and parenting simultaneously. Shooting from the gut he called Melody, "Hey. I need your help. Paul is gone and I'm looking for someone to take care of Becky when I'm working. Any ideas?"

She said, "What about me?"

Warren grinned at her response. He had hoped Melody would go for this. She continued, "What happened with Paul?"

"I don't want to get into it, and I don't know when he's coming back."

"Have you ever taken care of an infant?"

"Sort of. I helped my mom with my much younger brother. Plus, remember I worked for Mrs. Solomon when I was in high school, helping with her kids. But I always wanted to be a mother. Of course, it's not going to happen. I don't have the right equipment." Warren had almost forgotten that Melody was born a man and transitioned to a woman in her late teens. She had been a competent worker and he trusted her with the responsibility of childcare. How hard could it be? Paul figured it out so Melody should be able to.

And a jolt of Becky's crying halted the call as Warren rushed upstairs, panicking as to how he would stop her tears. He scooped the miracle from the crib, careful to hold her head, and gently fastened Becky to his chest and shoulder. He cradled a fragment of his wife, Rebecca. The paraphernalia strewn on the changing table, double dresser, and tall chest puzzled Warren. He talked into his iPhone and asked Alexa what to do.

Chapter 28
Paul

Paul's liberation from the shackles of the caretaking of Becky and Warren was complete. His plan to journey back to West Hollywood and crash in his old boyfriend Joshua's apartment had begun.   He succeeded in leaving Ocean Garden undetected by Warren. Joshua would need to temporarily bail Paul out. He had been the only man that he had had a splinter of a relationship with until Paul solidified his relationship with Warren. He pondered what would have happened if he had told Joshua he loved him and they had lived together. In the past year with Joshua, their uncomfortable connection had evolved into intense friendship.

He phoned Joshua, "Can I stay at your apartment until I get my bearings? I left Warren."

"What? Who is going to take care of your daughter? Are you nuts?"

"I had to leave. It was an impossible situation. I'll tell you everything when I get to your place. Just tell me if I can stay at your place."

"Yes. You'll have to sleep on the couch. I have a roommate in the second bedroom."

"Thank you. I'm on my way."

Paul ignored the incessant iPhone vibrations from Warren. Let him swelter in the obligations of caring for Becky, running the townhouse and his office. The herpes had nailed his decision to leave. How could he trust Warren?

Upon entering Joshua's apartment, he rallied up to his old life. There would be barhopping from The Rage to Mickey's, auditioning at Celebration Theater, and brunch at Eat Well on Santa Monica Boulevard. He would be an animal prowling for new conquests with his owl eyes.

Joshua's rent-controlled apartment changed little from Paul's last visit. Paul imagined the old lumpy pink couch and dining room table with unmatched chairs that had been collected from the thrift store Out of The Closet. The futon they used for sex sat in the corner. Paul's back would have an aerobic workout sleeping on that sofa or futon. The only alteration was Joshua's bedroom which housed a queen size bed. Paul had no intention of sleeping with Joshua. Paul asked, "What's going on with your political career?"

"Excellent, and I love living here. I even gave up my car. Everything I need is within walking distance."

A pang of jealousy rippled through Paul. The gay sensibility and easy unburdened lifestyle were a sharp contrast to Santa Monica.

"What's the deal with this roommate? Anything I should know?"

"Just roommates. His name is Barth. I hardly ever see him because he's a workaholic like Warren, an orthopedic nurse at St. Mitchells."

A short embrace before Paul updated Joshua on his soap opera, "I've been such an idiot. Warren is like a typical straight guy. He's hiding behind this phony supportive attitude while he expects me to do everything. I never should have gotten involved."

"But you said you loved him. That is big time for you, never being able to express that kind of emotion with anyone."

"You know, he's the one that wanted a child. I wasn't interested. He wanted a piece of Rebecca. I guess it wasn't enough that he had me. He wanted a little Rebecca."

"But Paul, you've been so exceptional as a father. You're always telling me you love Becky."

"Yes, yes. I'm so torn. I feel trapped. Like I've lost myself, whom I used to be."

"So, what's your plan?"

Paul replied, "No plans except I start teaching tomorrow. It's not enough to live on, so I've got to get something else. Maybe go back to IHC."

"I've got a Democratic Club meeting now; if you want, we can go out later. Maybe go to the beer bust at The Motherlode? Anyway, here's an extra set of keys."

Joshua's leaving gave Paul a chance to regroup. He went to the bathroom and looked at his face. The beginning of small lines at the corner of his eyes snapped back. And his pale skin looked fleshy, as though he had gained weight. *Is this what thirty-six years feels and looks like?* It felt like an eternity since he worked out at the gym. That would be his afternoon destination. A long visit to the sauna would release the toxins in his pores.

He took his satchel with a change of clothes he'd packed from Ocean Garden and headed towards the gym. The cruisy walk on Westbourne to Santa Monica Boulevard was 180 degrees from the more closeted Santa Monica. Paul had been awarded a get-out-of-jail card. A duty-free day to take care of himself. He could disregard texts with his iPhone powered off. He would stretch his muscles in Pilates class and cycle on the stationary gym bike.

Two men and a stroller confronted Paul as he headed south on Westbourne. In West Hollywood, strollers were often used as transport for small dogs. Without checking the contents Paul's curiosity asked, "How long have you had him?"

The man laughed and said, "Six months, and it's a baby girl."

His partner said, "We should have a sign saying child on board, not an animal."

Paul couldn't resist staring at the child with pink booties and a rainbow beachball topknot cap. Paul had to restrain himself from imagining walking with Warren and Becky. *Shit, it's less than a day and I already miss them.*

He jogged the remainder of the way to divert his mixed-message brain waves. The WeHo hallowed institution of body worshipers contrasted with the sedate Diamond Fitness Center in Ocean Park. Paul kept his head to the ground, not wanting to acknowledge his aging body compared to the under-thirty crowd. His muscles rebelled during the Pilates class, forcing him to bow out after a half hour. Cycling came easier and his aerobic heartbeat went through the five zones that included recovery and lactate threshold, which he had no clue as to what that was. He entered a thought-free zone for an hour.

Paul took his sweat-drenched body into the dry sauna. He hydrated himself with the consumption of a quart of water. Flashbacks of encounters he had had in this space begged him to realize how much he had changed from a slutty boy to a supposedly responsible man. His endorphins and testosterone were on high alert. The scarce afternoon crowd let him have enough space to lay down on the wooden sauna bench. The intense heat made him doze off.

The deep voice saying, "You know it's dangerous to sleep in here," awakened Paul. Paul felt dizzy when he tried to sit up after lying on the wooden bench. The man rescued Paul by offering him a jug of water. "Careful, you might be dehydrated."

Paul replied, "I drank before I entered." Paul guessed that the shaved-headed man with a slightly extended stomach bordered on forty-something. The freedom of meeting a stranger without clothes gave them a chance to appreciate each other's bodies. Not being judged by clothing was liberating.

"My name is Henry. Haven't seen you before?"

"Yeh, I'm usually in Santa Monica."

"Yes, it's kind of wild here. You have beautiful legs."

Paul panicked, "I'm in a relationship."

"Whoa, I'm just complimenting your legs. This isn't a pickup."

"Sorry, I'm in a weird place."

Henry moved across from Paul and began playing with his cock while he stared back at Paul. God, in the old days, Paul would participate with no qualms. He felt like he was in a distorted echo chamber. Dizziness stopped Paul from leaving.

Once he had recovered, Paul took a scrubbing shower and prided himself in keeping his sexual distance from the other members as he jogged back to Joshua's. A daily run would have to be enough exercise to keep his body toned.

While he was watching the Netflix series, *Orange is the New Black*, he fell asleep. His sleep was scuttled by Joshua and his guest traipsing through the living room. Paul tried to block the sounds escaping from Joshua's bedroom. A cluster-fuck evening that would leave Paul sapped of energy if he could not return to sleep. He could not afford to be a jitterbug on his first day of school.

Paul hoped that teaching classes in Santa Monica would give him respite, stopping him from obsessing about Warren and Becky. Thankfully, the following two weeks of teaching, since he had left Ocean Garden, did the trick.

During his daily jog, he heard his name called.

"Hey, Paul. Don't run off." The face hadn't registered with Paul until he realized it was the actor, William, with a beard, from *P.S. Your Cat is Dead.*

"William, right? Hi. I didn't recognize you."

"I'm doing a part in some online series that doesn't pay much but at least I'll get exposure. I have to play a fifty-year-old and growing a beard seemed to be an easy way to get that look."

Paul's body was craving nourishment from William. He wanted to wrestle with this bearded animal. Yet, how could he justify this crime against Warren and Becky? He attempted to back off until William grabbed his hand, and after he nibbled Paul's ear, Paul surrendered.

"Hey Paul, what do you want to do?"

"Go back to my apartment on Westbourne."

During the walk, William rambled about his acting jobs while Paul morphed into his sexual marauder character. Before they entered the apartment, William's dark odor wrapped Paul into a frenzy. Paul and William slashed off their 501 jeans and began mauling each other. Paul had forgotten what having a fuck for fuck's sake felt like while they were grinding against the hardwood floor. Within seconds Paul paused. He conjured a beam shining from a lighthouse through a zero-visibility fog. Immobilized, he shriveled when he became choked up with, *I'm a father. I have a lover. I have purpose. I don't need this. I'm not going to jeopardize my relationship with the only man I've ever said, "I love you" to. How could I have abandoned Becky?* Paul disentangled from William, lifted himself from the floor and pulled his jeans on.

William said, "You okay, Paul?"

"Yes. I'm sorry. I thought this is what I wanted. Guess not."

William realized the evening was over and told Paul, "Don't worry about tonight. It was good to connect anyway. Maybe I'll see you at the theater." Relief seized Paul that William was a *mensch* and did not create a scene about the bungled evening and mixed messages that Paul had given him.

William left and a cycle of agitation slammed Paul, *I'm ashamed of myself. Warren will never forgive. He won't understand if I cheated despite what he told me.* Paul's twitching body kept searching for a cavernous sleep, trying to ignore the cement futon and his congested thoughts that barricaded him. At four a.m. his brain gave up wrestling.

Chapter 29
Stretched Love

Warren reorganized his schedule to accommodate Becky as his number one priority. Delegating tasks to Teresa was liberating. During the week, the bond with Becky brought him within emotional walking distance of Rebecca. A miniature version of Rebecca, a helpless creation that needed his life force. Warren's battery got charged when he tickled Becky's toes. Her giggles brought Rebecca's voice to the walls of the townhouse. Warren remembered Rebecca's laughter when his fingers crept along her feet. Rebecca would joke, "You're making me laugh so hard I'm going to have an accident." The primal activity was a building block in their relationship and he wanted Becky to squeal like Rebecca. Warren found that tickling was a way of social bonding. Becky wet herself during the tickling session but Warren didn't mind changing the diaper. A connection between Becky and Rebecca and himself. During the rediapering, he said, "Becky, you know you are just like Rebecca. I love you so much. Daddy is going to take care of you." Her smile initiated an electric current that traveled throughout his body.

Having Melody split her time between the office and Ocean Garden gave Warren confidence he wouldn't get overwhelmed. But no communication with Paul left a gaping hole in his chest that caused him to feel his emotional pain. A disoriented Warren functioned but craved the trembling love he felt when Paul held him.

Before Warren settled Rebecca into her crib she vocalized, "Daddy." Was he hallucinating? At eight months, had Becky really grasped language? Warren's parents told him nothing came out of his mouth beyond baby talk until he was eighteen months old. He blamed the organic food and formula for Becky's magic-talking trick. Warren pulled out his iPhone and captured the Kodak moment with the sound of his daughter speaking her first words. Even with this milestone, Warren felt brutalized going to sleep without Paul. *How can I still love him after his abandoning me and Becky?*

That following morning, the smell of freshly ground Peet coffee beans crept into the bedroom. He didn't remember setting the predetermined timer last night. The Keurig must have a mind of its own or Rebecca was haunting him. The audio from the nursery confirmed that Becky was sleeping soundly. Warren shaved and showered vigorously, recalling the miraculous sound of *Daddy* that Becky uttered the previous day.

Warren entered the dark nursery quietly. Near the crib, Paul was curled in the fetal position sleeping on the floor. Warren rubbed his eyes to ensure he wasn't dreaming or creating a mirage in his head. He bent down to Paul's level and kissed his forehead

"She said 'Daddy.'"

Paul dragged Warren to the floor, kissed his mouth and then cuddled in his arms. Fifteen minutes later the stirring from Becky awakened Paul and Warren. Paul ached to hold Becky. He realized *the last two weeks were the only time I haven't held our daughter daily since she was born.* When he reached for Becky, Warren was wrapped behind him just as Becky said, "Daddy." The joyful weeping had no boundaries for Paul, Warren or Becky. Ocean Garden was whole again, and they imagined that Rebecca had a prideful smile. Love had stretched and become elastic.

About the Author

During 2020, Gordon had published work in Whoa Nelly Press, Wingless Dreamer, Two Hawks Quarterly, the Santa Monica College Journals Chronicles and On-Going Moments, and Gay Wicked Ways. Gordon participated in the filming of *Queers Across the Years* as a writer and performer. Ten of his autobiographical stories are available on the Queer Slam Episode 21, podcast called "Just Gordon." Gordon wrote and performed in *Queerly Imparted* at the Skylight Theater in Los Angeles as part of the World AIDS Day celebration. In February 2023, his play *Reflections* was chosen and presented at the Region 8 KCACTF festival in Las Vegas, Nevada.

Other Books written by Gordon Blitz

Shipped Off

Fathers and Other Strangers